Time and Tide

A COLLECTION OF TALES

SANDRA WILLIAMS

γνῶθι σεαυτόν

Cover Design: Xavier Bertolotti - www.graphistemetz.com
Cover Image: Old Garden Beach - Robert Louis Williams
www.robertlouiswilliams.com

PERMISSIONS

Excerpt from "Preface to a Twenty Volume Suicide Note" in S O S: POEMS *1961-2013*, © 2014 by The Estate of Amiri Baraka, by permission from Grove/Atlantic, Inc. Any third party use of this material, outside of this publication, is prohibited.

Excerpt from "A Star Without a Name" by Jalāl ad-Dīn Muhammad Rūmī (Mathnawi III, 1284-1288), translation by Coleman Barks in *Say I Am You*, (© Maypop, 1994), by express permission from Coleman Barks. Any third party use of this material, outside of this publication, is prohibited.

Excerpt from "Faith" by David Whyte in *River Flow: New & Selected Poems*, by permission from Many Rivers Press, www.davidwhyte.com. ©Many Rivers Press, Langley, WA 98260 USA. Any third party use of this material, outside of this publication, is prohibited.

Time and Tide: a collection of tales is a work of fiction. Names, characters and incidents were created by the author and/or are used fictiously. Any resemblance to actual events and persons, living or deceased, is entirely coincidental.

ISBN-13:978-0692941690 (Sono)
ISBN-10:069294169X

γνῶθι σεαυτὸν
SONO PUBLICATIONS
Rockport, Massachusetts

Dedication

Mary Ann Wells, dear friend,
kindred spirit, kind, generous soul,
you are sorely missed.

BY THE SAME AUTHOR

Moss On Stone: a historical novella

Standing under the stars
tide coming in
I am reminded—
parts of me are missing
I can not name the
fragments of my self—
out there somewhere
in time or tide
so near but
deeper than I can reach

~SANDRA WILLIAMS

Contents

Book of Hours
Of the inspiration for the tales

The sign catches her eye. It is round and gleaming in the late afternoon sun: TIME & TIDE ANTIQUE CLOCKS above a white clock face with black Roman numerals. She notices there are no hands on the clock. Although the shop has been on the outskirts of town forever, she had never taken notice of it as she does on this day. Having driven two hours from the Philadelphia airport, she is ready for the day to end, yet she is compelled to turn at the entrance next to the sign.

Helen has been twenty years away from the sights and sounds of Lancaster County, Pennsylvania. Memory awakens in a dreamlike way, as she observes the horse and buggies clopping along the roads, and the makeshift farm stands stocked with fall wares: chrysanthemums and pumpkins lining the front, jars of relish and jam stacked on shelves, zinnias and dahlias in tin buckets.

She stops to buy flowers for her mother. A sullen young girl in a plain gingham dress and white apron, who makes no eye contact, lifts a bunch of bright zinnias and wraps them in newspaper. She hands them to Helen, counts out change from a green glass jar and returns to her post.

Driving on past the field of sunflowers, Helen remembers how, when she was a child, she would stand

1

at her window for hours, gazing at the endless acres to watch them turn their brown eyes toward the sun's arc across the sky. The variegated crops in patches, like a giant quilt, stretch over the landscape to the misty blue hills beyond. Despite the quaint appeal and simple beauty of the place, she feels she's been washed ashore on a lonely island—as a stranger.

Just a few weeks ago, she received the letter. Her mother was dying. She had to come, wanted to come. During those years away, she hadn't thought to return, not even for a visit, but here she is now in the place that had never felt like home. She found her true home in the Mediterranean—on the island of Lipari, bathed in light and warmth, wrapped in blue sea and sky. She intends to carry something of it with her into the cold winter ahead, which holds the unwelcome promise of grief.

Time is of the essence. This she knows, but there *will* be time with her mother before it is too late. Still, she turns at the sign instead of going the short distance to the bleak farmhouse where her mother lies waiting.

She drives slowly past a white-washed mansion with an ornate wrought iron fence, brick walkway lined with hedge rows and Victorian lamp posts. Though the elegance of the stately house seems out of place in the otherwise austere landscape dotted with modest houses, it gratifies her finer sensibilities.

Just ahead she spots a long, concrete block building,

assuming it is the shop, though there are no signs or markings on it. With some effort, she pulls open the carved wooden door that looks like a portal to a church rather than to the one-story rectangular warehouse. When she steps over the threshold, out of the bright afternoon daylight into what seems total darkness, she hesitates. The interior slowly comes into focus as sun shafts filter down from row of windows along the top of the building. She moves into the misty light to the sound of ticking clocks. *Such an odd place,* she thinks, as her vision adjusts to take in the sight of hundreds of clocks on multi-leveled shelves set on long tables. Amid the odor of wood and dampness, she sees no one, not even at the island desk far ahead that seems to mark the middle of the gaunt space.

She walks an unhurried pace along the main aisle, and several side aisles, viewing the vast display of clocks standing like old soldiers at attention, waiting to be inspected. She stops here and there noting their shapes and designs. She admires the colorful ceramic clocks with scenes of farmhouses and gardens. She shudders at the somber black cases of others. She smiles at the one with a white marble base, a brass horse and hound on one side, and bright yellow clock face under a glass dome on the other.

Where have these clocks been, and what have they seen? Who were their owners, and how had they lived? Where are the souls now who lived by their ringing reminders of passing time? She wonders.

She is startled to hear a thin voice in familiar sing-song Pennsylvania Dutch. Turning, she sees an old man standing next to her, as if he has just appeared out of the mist.

"Can I help you?"

"Oh, thanks, but…no, no, I just popped in to see what you have here. I grew up in this town, but I'd never been to your shop."

"Welcome, then, but it's not my shop, Miss. It's my father's."

Your father's? she thinks, but says only, "Oh?"certain that his father could not possibly still be alive. The man looks ancient, bent over, with white wispy hair, and eyes clouded with a bluish film.

"You let me know if you have any questions, young lady."

"I will for sure. Thank you."

"Marchenmeister"

"Excuse me?"

"Marchenmeister, I'm Earl Marchenmeister, Jr."

"Oh, right…yes. Well, nice to meet you, Earl. I'm Helen. I think I'll just take a quick look around if that's okay."

"Yah, you do that, Miss Helen. I'll be right there," pointing to the island ahead situated in the sea of clocks. She watches as he pads his way back to the elaborate desk, its front in the shape of a ship's prow.

What a strange little man!

She imagines that over the years he has cared for every timepiece, recognizes each unique chime or bell, knows where each has been, maybe even the fate of those who had owned it. She wonders if he has a son who will inherit the shop from *him* when his time runs out.

Now I am being ridiculous; he's just an old-fashioned man who's inherited the shop, and still thinks of it as his father's. Why do I care about that? What does it matter to me? No matter!

Then she sees it—an exact replica of the clock in her apartment in Italy—elegant with a satiny red cherry wood case embellished with gold leaf designs. The hands on the clock face are filigreed silver, and a flowery scarlet line is drawn around the perimeter above the hours. On the glass door, in the thinnest of gold lines, is drawn an image of the basilica of Santa Croce in Florence. The embossed silver pendulum peeks through, swaying hypnotically, as she is lost in disbelief.

Helen had been a wayfarer ever since she can remember—first in thought. Then, restless and curious, she left home and wandered for years on end, traveling through the Greek isles and Italy. Finally, she settled in Florence, across from the Piazza di Santa Croce on via di San Giuseppe, thinking she had found a home. She was thrilled to have had a few feature articles published in *La Nationale's* series on "Americans in Tuscany," and a few short stories in European magazines. And, she had found love she thought was lasting. She felt she was living a dream, all of her senses heightened. But one day, her lover left—without a word. Again she was alone and restless.

When she saw the ad: "appartamento con vista," on Lipari, one of the Aeolian Islands off of Sicily, she did not hesitate for a moment. Before she had even set foot on the island, a view from the ferry confirmed that she had found a home at last. Before a month had passed, she had settled in to devote herself to writing and continued to submit short stories to the few small European publishing houses expressing interest.

As soon as she entered the apartment, she saw it on the mantel above the fireplace, an exquisite clock with the image of Santa Croce drawn in delicate gold lines on the glass over a pendulum formed like a labyrinth. To her it was another affirmation that she belonged, bringing the past into the future. She had arrived after so many harried years in search of a place she could call home.

As she settled in, when the clock chimed, often she would close eyes and feel herself back in Florence—her lover warm beside her on the daybed by the fire, his kind and shining eyes looking upon her, the smell of espresso and wood fire drifting in through the window, church bells resounding through the room.

❧

With thoughts of the Mediterranean, whose beauty still surprises her after so many years, she is warmed now in the cold warehouse, but dislocated by the appearance of the familiar clock. She crosses the aisle to gaze at it for a time in reverie. Then she turns to make her way to the desk where the old man is dozing with arms folded across his chest.

"Excuse me...excuse me, Earl," she whispers, so as not to wake him.

He opens his eyes and looks up, "You want to know something about one of my clocks?"

"Yes, yes, I do have a question. I saw that beautiful Italian clock just down the aisle there. At least I think it's Italian. I have one exactly like it. I mean...it isn't mine. It was there in my apartment in Italy when I moved in, and .... " They walk together to where the clock rests.

"Oh, this one," Earl remarks. "This is special, Miss Helen, one of a kind it is. There are no others."

Just as Helen begins to protest, eager to assure the old man there *is* a replica she has lived with for many years, all of the clocks begin their hourly fugue of chimes and bells. When the ringing finally plays out and fades to uneven ticking, she speaks more loudly than needed.

"No others? That can't be. There must be..."

"No, one of a kind it is. Yah, this is a special one."

"One of a kind? No, it's exactly like the one I.... How long has it been here?"

"Hmm, can't remember how long now. From New England it came...maybe twenty years ago? Maybe waiting just for you, no?"

"No, it must have...." She takes a deep breath, then asks, "Can you tell me something about it? It must have..."

"The clocks will tell you about themselves."

"What? What do you mean? How, how do they tell about themselves?"

"When they are yours and you love them, you hear what they know."

"Know? What? Then *you* must have heard what this clock knows, right?"

"Yah, yah, but it's different for everyone, Miss Helen. Yah, you will see."

"This is all very strange," shaking her head, still in disbelief.

Earl turns from the clock to face Helen, "Yah, different, but not so strange. You will see."

"See? How will I...?" Feeling a bit strange herself, it is clear the old man is not going to tell her a thing about the clock. "I will think about it. It's lovely, but I...I should be going now." Heading toward the door, she turns for a last glimpse of the clock, feeling she is abandoning it— silencing it somehow.

"Not going to take it with you now, Miss Helen?" Earl calls after her, his last words rising in a raspy voice. "It will have things to tell you."

Who is that man anyway, the Geppetto of clocks?

She shakes her head again and laughs, picking up her pace. Pushing hard on the heavy door, she is expecting a burst of light, but the sun is already low on the horizon.

When she arrives at her mother's house, Mary, a hospice nurse, answers the door, holding out her hand in greeting. "Helen? Nice to finally meet you. How was your trip? You must have had a few very long days."

"Mary? Good to meet you too. Yes, a long few days, but all went well. Thank you so much for keeping in touch, and for...everything you've done."

"Not at all, I wanted to wait until you arrived."

"I apologize. I should have gotten here sooner. How is she?"

"No worries, really, I didn't mind. She's asleep now, but has been restless all day, looking forward to welcoming you home. I told her she would see you when she wakes up. That made her smile."

"Do you think I could wake her?"

"Well, I've just given her morphine for comfort and rest. She may not rouse easily, but you can certainly try."

Mary shows Helen how to administer morphine drops for anxiety or pain, and how to set up the nebulizer for breathing treatments. "I'll be back day after tomorrow, but you'll call me if you have any questions, or...if things take a turn for the worse, won't you?"

"Yes, will do." Helen walks with Mary to the door, thanks her again and says good night.

"Good night, Helen...and welcome home."

Walking through the hall to the kitchen, Helen looks around.

Home. Nothing's changed; everything's changed.

She places the zinnias in a Mason jar she finds on the dusty window sill. She goes to her bag to get the gift she's brought for her mother, and turns into the dining room, set up for care of the old woman who rests in the dim and close room.

So thin and frail. Oh, Mother, I should have come sooner.

She sets the flowers on the bedside table. Leaning over, she touches her mother's slender arm, and takes her blue-veined hand into her own

"Mother, it's me. It's Helen."

"Helen?"

"Yes, I'm here now"

"I've been waiting," her mother whispers back. Her eyes drift to the ceiling, flutter and close again from the effort.

"I know, I know, Mother, I'm here now, and look, I've brought you something."

Helen positions a large mosaic tile under the lamplight on the dresser across from the bed. The scene of Lipari in the sea is illuminated: red tile roofs, golden bell towers and tall cypress trees on azure hills.

"Look, Mother, isn't it lovely?"

The old woman opens her eyes and looks long at the tile. She smiles. "Bring it to me," her voice fading into a sigh.

Helen holds the tile so her mother can see it, then sets it next to the flowers. She sits at the bedside, her eyes on the slight figure now in a sound sleep, and holds the hand of the woman who had been strong, so severe, so demanding.

She did the best she could. That's all anyone can ask...all anyone can be expect, isn't it?

The weight of guilt and grief about to descend, Helen rises, steps into the hall, picks up her bag and climbs the stairs to the little room at the top.

She is taken aback, but not entirely surprised, to see that there too everything is as it had been when she left at age eighteen: high school banner above the mirror; jewelry box on the dresser; some forgotten trinkets; faded pictures of Einstein and Leonard Cohen on the cork board over the white and gold provincial desk. She slides the dusty board behind the dresser and stuffs everything else into one of its empty drawers. When she looks into the mirror, she half expects to see the younger version of herself reflected back.

Has it really been twenty years?

She sees that Mary has left clean linens for the bed under the dormer, and a forgotten multi-color quilt her mother had made for her sixteenth birthday. Helen runs her hand over the Joseph's Coat pattern. She turns on the bedside lamp in the shape of a sunflower, hoping the warm light will fill the dreary room, and the empty feeling within.

Exhaustion setting in, she quickly makes up the bed, and from her bag she takes a small embroidered pillow, a silk melon flower and a book of hours—familiar things she knows will settle a rising tide of sadness and unease.

Three things about the book always comfort her: Each page is bordered in gold with designs of ivy intertwined with bright cornflowers, daisies, columbine and wild strawberries. Second, there are twelve small illustrations—jewel-like vignettes of peasants going about their monthly labors, and third, the prayers and verses designated for hours of day and night.

Although she does not consider herself religious, she had been drawn to the practice of reading from the book when the church bells rang out at the canonical hours across every Italian town and village. She carries it to the window, opens the sash and reads the verse for the end of day into the cold silence, the moon rising above the dark fields below.

When at last she lies on the bed, her thoughts turn to the clock shop, half wondering if it disappeared as she drove away: the stately house, the warehouse full of clocks and the odd figure of the man inside, with his claim that the clocks stand ready to tell what they know. At least, if that familiar clock were near, she might feel closer to her island home—another comfort. Though she does not believe that the clock could tell her anything, she doesn't entirely disbelieve it either.

Helen dozes off and on throughout the night, getting up several times to check on her mother. She is in a deep sleep in the morning though when she is awakened by the sound of her mother coughing. She bolts out of bed and down the stairs.

"Mother, I'm here. Are you okay?" Leaning down, she kisses her mother's cheek and reaches for her hand. The coughing becomes so intense and lasts so long, it frightens her. She goes for the morphine, takes the liquid up into a dropper, opens her mother's lips with one hand, and with the other empties a few drops onto her tongue. When the coughing subsides, the old woman opens her eyes, and turns her head toward the mosaic tile and bright zinnias.

She looks at her daughter and smiles, "Helen?"

"I'm here, Mother. Do you remember, I came in last night? Mary told me you're doing well," Helen lies, "and what I need to do to take care of you. Here, let me fluff your pillow." She straightens the covers, and sets up the nebulizer. "I'm going to make you some hot tea and toast."

When she returns with a tea tray, she removes the inhaler. The old woman opens one eye and moves her lips as if trying to form words. Helen hears only unintelligible sounds.

"What are you saying, Mother?" Again, the whispered sounds, and then a third utterance. Helen feels desperate to interpret what her mother is trying to say, but to no avail.

"I love you too," she hears herself say, choosing to believe her mother's words had been, "I love you," although they had never before been spoken to Helen.

She senses her mother drifting off to a place further away than sleep, her breathing becoming heavy with a watery sound. She carries the tray into the kitchen and returns to hear the breathing is now a loud gurgling.

A call to Mary confirms, "It may be the dying process has begun," Mary says and offers to come, but Helen refuses.

Dying process? No, not already, not so soon. She does not want to believe the hour has come. If they had more time together, her mother might have said, "I missed you so, Helen," and asked, "Why did you stay away so long?" She recalls that, on the flight back, she was hoping they would not have that tiresome conversation again. Now she wishes they were able to talk about that—or anything.

"I told you before, Mother," she would have said. "I found a home in Italy, and my work is there."

Was there, that is. I have nothing to write, nothing to say, believing for some time now that she has no stories left to tell and no inspiration in sight.

She once heard a best-selling author say, "I have a million stories in my head, and I'll never have enough time to write them all."

Helen does not have even one, and believes she never will again.

All through this day she reads to her mother from the book of hours, to the sound of that breathing she will never forget. She thinks of her mother's smile when she saw the mosaic tile as both a welcome home and a blessing on the life she had chosen, if not forgiveness for having left her mother alone.

Toward evening, the breathing fades into silence as Helen reads the verse for vespers:

What man of you, having a hundred sheep, if he lose one of them, doth not leave the ninety and nine in the wilderness, and go after that which is lost, until he find it? And when he hath found it, he layeth it on his shoulders, rejoicing. And when he cometh home, he calleth together his friends and neighbors, saying unto them, Rejoice with me; for I have found my sheep which was lost.

Phone calls are made, a funeral arranged, a memorial service planned, a burial endured. Now, there are the legal and financial obligations, and the ritual of sorting through the things in the house, and the things in her heart.

The mementos Helen's mother held dear: a ceramic

rose candy dish, a framed cross stitch of an Amish boy, a figurine of a glittery angel, had never meant anything to Helen—until now. There are boxes of yellowed papers in closets, pictures, cards and letters in a desk drawer—ones she had sent her mother over the years. On a snowy evening, she burns them in the fireplace, envisioning the resentments and regrets in the house, and within her, rising up into the clean, cold air above.

⁊

Through the months of winter, Helen lives in the quiet house filled with the absence of her mother and thoughts of her years of waiting and loneliness. Now *she* lives in loneliness with the lingering dread that inspiration for her work is gone forever—that which has always sustained her and kept her from despair. At night she lies in the cold room at the top of the stairs, listening to the wind whip around house—the house she thought she had escaped from, an ocean away from the light and blue of Lipari.

Then, one early February morning before sunrise, Helen feels a turning within. She will move her bed and few belongings to the front room downstairs, where the southern exposure allows the light of the lengthening days. There she will have a fire to warm her in the evenings.

When all is in place, she takes the book of hours from whee it had remained since the night of her mother's death. She opens it to find the miniature depiction of the labor for February: a peasant woman at a beehive holding a honeycomb. She places the open book on a table and lights votive candles, which burn until dawn. That day, Helen returns to the clock shop, and again walks the long aisles.

She stops at the place where she thought she had seen the Italianate clock. It's not there. She walks half the length of the shop to the desk, expecting to find the old man napping.

Oh, Here it is!

At the counter behind the desk the clock is waiting, its pendulum keeping time. A calm comes over her and, at the same time, a feeling of awakening from a long sleep. Seemingly out of nowhere, a voice is heard.

"You've come for your clock then," more statement than question. "It's ready to go."

When she turns toward the voice, she sees, not the old man, but a much younger one. She notices he does not have the local accent and does not look like he belongs in what she has come to think of as, *that fairy tale of a shop.*

"Oh, yes…actually, I did come to see if the clock was still here, but…where's the old man, Earl? How did he….How did you know I'd be back?"

"*I'm* Earl, Earl, Jr., remember?" he says, as he places the clock into a wooden box. "I'm trying to keep the shop going, but there isn't much interest or demand these days." It's just me here now. My father died a few years ago.

A few years ago? "No, it was only…." Helen feels she will melt away. Light headed and confused, the tranquility on first seeing the clock dissolves in an instant. "What? I mean, when I was here before, the old man…he and I talked. I can see how he thought I might be back, but I don't understand. That was only a few *months* ago."

The young man smiles. "That was *me*, Miss Helen, remember? You spoke to *me* that day. We did talk about the clock, and I knew you would be back because you loved it. Well, no matter! Here you are now, and you will have what you came for."

"No matter? It was *not* you. It was the old man. He said it was his father's shop. Am I dreaming or…?"

"We are all dreaming, no?"

"Yes…no, not now, but I … "

"Here you are, Miss. This is a special one; it's yours now," holding out the box to her. For just a moment, she is drawn into his gaze.

It's all so strange, but in a way familiar now, his smile, his kind and shining eyes, and the clock.

Neither one speaks a word. She takes the box, holds it close to her and walks toward the door, having the same thought she had when she had left the shop the first time, seemingly a lifetime ago now.

Will it all vanish into thin air when it is out of my sight?

She walks out into that silent stillness before a snowfall.

The clock is beautiful, glowing above the blazing fireplace in the little room. She runs her fingers over the case, tracing the golden lines on the glass. She spends days in reverie there—*what to do, where to go—back or forward?* She doesn't know, but, for now, she will simply live in its silent company.

On the threshold of spring, she awakens as if preparing to sail out on a faraway adventure. She takes up the key, winds the clock and sets the pendulum into motion. In the following days, she reads the designated prayers at the hours of daylight, and often during the night. As the chimes sound, she sometimes feels herself drifting into another realm of no place or time.

There, at peace, she remains until all manner of dark and light beings began to flash and flutter before her —some in images like holographs, others heard in voices, heard in whispers and secret thoughts. When they come, they come like a swift, incoming tide—surreal, filled with beauty and sadness, old regrets and new life, muddled, intertwined, as in a dream.

There is an image of a man come back to his childhood home to tell his story to an empty room, and the voice of a woman obsessed with the starry sky brought back to earth through the suffering of others. She thinks the thoughts of a therapist whose saintly lover leaves her a gift, and of a husband left alone to endure memories of all that is lost to him. She sees the shadow of an enlightened soul becoming a truer form of herself. She hears a mother grieving for her lost son on sacred ground. She experiences the confusion of a young actress who is deceived by desire for what she thought she loved. There is the vision of a teacher whose broken, irreparable things become her strength.

Are these the beings who once owned the clock, lost in time—waiting to tell their tales? Are they conjured out of Helen's revived imagination? Or do they emanate from the eternal minds of distant souls who, like the Greek hero Odysseus, found ways of contending with the trials they encountered—wandering on their way home to a place of rest?

Not each day, nor all at once, but over the course of a year, she sees them, hears them, feels she *is* them. She dreams their dreams, is in the dreams—learns their minds —and their stories, hundreds of them, maybe enough to last a lifetime. She will speak as them and for them.

≈

Helen returns to her azure island home, having come to rest in her love for the beings and the truth of their stories she carries inside her. She sits by the window, gazing once again upon the turquoise sea, and begins to write them down—one by one.

The Tales

The Holes They Leave

Of a woman obsessed with the starry sky

That night the stars kept me awake. I couldn't sleep, so I went to the window overlooking the ocean. A green light flashed at the horizon beyond the cloaked meadow. Looking up, I saw more stars than I ever remember, brilliant and shimmering. Elated, I felt my whole being inhaling the ebony sky teeming with star life. I stood in awe for moments, minutes, or hours—how long, I can't say.

When I returned to my bed, I still couldn't sleep, but not because of the mad convergence of memories, desires and fears that had been crowding in on me before. My mind was free, pure with the light of those gems in the dark velvet sky. I wasn't drawn back to look again, however compelling; rather, I just rested in quiet wakefulness, letting the stars live, expand in me—as they always were and always will be.

But not long enough. As the first light dawned, edging in on me was an awareness of my own smallness against the expanse of the grandeur I had witnessed. I wished to remain in that blessed state, like one holding on to a fading dream, but those habitual, chaotic thoughts began pressing in once more: the absurdity of being human, the perpetual dirge sounding beneath the surface of mundane reality. I felt an impending void. I wanted to fill it with the beauty and mystery of the starry heavens. Out there, in here, *"as above, so below,"* these words were like pearls on the strand of my desire to remain as I had been, but it was not to be.

That was the night the stars kept me awake.

Since then, I haven't been the same. Why? I don't know, but I am determined to return to that state of grace. During the day, I go about my routine and practical matters, but with anticipation of the other half of my life— the night. It's all obsession. I sleep for an hour or two then awaken and wander to the window to see if the stars are as they had been that night. They never are.

I know it's crazy, but there has to be a way back. I began trying anything that might diminish my agitated condition. I've attempted to clear my mind through meditation, but to no avail. I bought a bunch of self-help books, joined a Yoga class, devour natural remedies for sleeplessness, anxiety and depression. I also started seeing a therapist, which I had meant to do when I came back from my travels a couple of years ago.

I am also reading poetry about the stars hoping to affirm my experience of that night. I've found many star-inspired expressions, but the lines in this poem come closest to my obsession to recreate it:

And now, each night I count the stars,
And each night I get the same number.
And when they will not come to be counted,
I count the holes they leave.

Desperate to find peace, and as a last-ditch effort, I asked my therapist to prescribe something to help me sleep. About a week into taking the meds, this happened: While asleep, I got up, went outside, walked into my next door neighbor's house, opened her refrigerator, took out a bowl of pasta and ate it. I also took her dog out for a walk, then wandered back to my place.

My neighbor Dana had witnessed the whole scene, and came over the next morning to tell me about my strange adventure. I didn't believe her—not until she showed me the evidence. When she heard me come in, she followed me around, began taking a video, watching in amazement, ready to call 911 in case things got even crazier. I was embarrassed, and it was frightening to hear. I felt like an idiot. So much for sleeping pills!

Dana and I went for a walk on the beach that afternoon. It was sunny and warm for late October, the sea all lapis lazuli and silver wrinkles under a clear sky. We talked as we walked into our elongated shadows. Until then, I had thought I didn't know her very well, but I realized today that I feel closer to her than to anyone. Even though, ashamed of the incident the night before, I feel safe with her, maybe because she had said more than once that I remind her of her daughter Linney, who had recently come home after years away.

I told her about the night the stars kept me awake, and my unshakable obsession. I even told her about the poetry I'd found that could sometimes calm me. I started to feel like Dana could see through to the real me. (I am not sure there is a real me.) I didn't resent it though; at least that would mean *someone* knew me. The thing is, I'd never confided in anyone before in that way (not even my therapist, not really). And Dana didn't think I was insane.

How can I say what it's like—my quest? Waiting for the new moon and cloudless sky, going down to the ocean's edge to stargaze in the "mystical moist night air" (another line from a poem). Even though the heavens are always majestic, there's never anything to catch me off guard—like on that night.

That's it!

Why am I always on guard? I ask myself. I have no answer. Poetry is the only thing that *can* catch me off guard—with ideas and feelings I've never had before, but I somehow recognize them as mine when I "hear" them— the beauty and truth of them. I find myself more at ease at those times, and a little less desperate.

My therapist tells me I *do* have the answer, and she will help me find it. Part of me thinks it's all bullshit: her reassurances, my quest, my questions, my obsession, my strategies and remedies. What would it mean to come to terms with an answer, if there is one? Still, I continue the therapy and all the rest of it (except the sleeping pills). Why? Because I want to get back to perfection—the ultimate distraction from myself—that feeling of the stars living in me.

A couple of weeks after Dana and I had walked together, she called to say we should meet for dinner. Her invitation made me feel good—comforted to think of being with her again. She said she had a gift for me, and I got the impression she also wanted to tell me something. I figure she has worried about me ever since the sleep-walking incident. I look forward to our meeting when I will confide in her even more—tell her things and ask her things.

She's a wise person, an "old soul," as they say. I respect and trust her. I will even let my guard down, intentionally this time and really spill my guts (poor Dana). Maybe I will hear myself say something that will surprise me, like poetry can, something that comes from the part of me that isn't on guard.

Driving back from a therapy session I decide I should just quit going. The therapist is bringing up stuff I don't want to think about, which I guess would be good, if I really want to get to the bottom of things? But it doesn't feel good, and besides, I am already at the bottom of… something, but also feel at a threshold.

As I pass Dana's house, I see a woman on the sidewalk with Dana's dog. It's a damp, raw November evening. Something is wrong. She's in a nightgown, pacing back and forth, looking like she's in a daze. It's got to be Dana's daughter. I pull up next to her and roll down the window.

"Are you okay? You're Dana's daughter, Linney, right?" She's crying, so I can barely make out what she's saying. She doesn't answer my question.

She just keeps repeating, "Mom, why? What am I gonna to do? Why, why did you do this to me?"

She doesn't even seem to notice me. I get out of the car and practically pick her up to get her into the back seat. The dog jumps in too. I tell her I'm her next door neighbor, and a friend of her mother's, which makes her cry even more. I bring her back to my place, clear a spot on the sofa and pour us both a shot of whisky. Between her sobs, I hear what's happened.

"My mother's dead," her voice strained."I didn't know…she…she …"

"What? No…" I interrupt, "No, that can't be true; we were supposed to…"

"Yes, yes it *is* true. She was sick, but she didn't even tell me. Do you believe that? I called to her last night, and when…when she didn't answer, I went into her room. I kept shaking her, but she didn't wake up. She didn't looked well, so I called an ambulance. I stayed with her until… until the end. It was horrible, and I… I…"

She begins crying again. I don't want to pressure her, so I just let her go on and get everything out. When the sobs subside, she tells me that Dana had regained consciousness at the hospital, but the doctors told Linney that her mother was in the end stage of Leukemia. She would not be coming home. There was just time enough time for goodbyes. That's when Dana told Linney about the things she had left for her. You'd think it would've been something for Linney to hold on to, but maybe that's harder—thinking about the only things left of a person who's never coming back.

"I'm not gonna to do it. I don't wanna see anything —whatever she left. I...I can't...I won't. Anyway, she... hated me and..."

I stop Linney right there, trying to set her straight, "Now, that is *not* true. Your mother did *not* hate you; she talked about you a lot. She wanted the best for you; she loved you." I didn't know much about their relationship, but I did know Dana worried about her.

"No, no she didn't," Linney practically screams at me, with a blank look, then puts her hands over her face, her body shaking in silent gasps. While I wait for her to calm, I realize she is probably about the same age as I am, but is quite a beauty. So Dana's saying I reminded her of Linney had nothing to do with our looking alike. She is a lot smaller and thinner (I try to ignore the sharp twinge of that fact). She has the kind of looks, no doubt, that turn a lot of heads, open a lot of doors, and maybe keep her from seeing herself as she really is.

I remember Dana told me that once Linney said, "I'm starving," and she knew it was literally true. So, she somehow persuaded her to go to lunch. Linney ordered crudités (which sounds a lot better than "raw vegetables"). Dana said they would have tasted better too, with the crab and cheddar dip. Apparently, Linney was frantic to move the vegetables away from the dip, "as if they were going to jump into it by themselves. The dip should have come with a ten-foot pole," was what Dana had said. She could be funny like that, but it was sad too, partly because I can relate to that kind of thinking big time.

Linney *was* like me in that she had been away a few years "traveling" (a kinder way of saying, "wandering") and came home, Dana had said, to sort things out and get her life back on track. I'm also waiting for that to happen for me.

After a few minutes of silence, I hear myself say, "You can stay here tonight, so you are not alone," but hope she doesn't take me up on it (until she doesn't). That's when I feel a dark and heavy weight looming, about to crash down. For some reason, she wants to sleep in her mother's bed, so I walk back with her and get her settled in with the dog.

The next morning I check in on her. She cries off and on, but doesn't say anything else about Dana's sudden "disappearance," avoids eye-contact, and keeps repeating, "I don't want to live in this house. I've gotta get away from here. I can't stay. I'm not going through those things she left. I'm just *not!* I'll go away. I don't want to see anything or look at anything."

Okay, okay already, what a big baby, I'm thinking. I only say, "Your mother must have had her reasons—leaving certain things for you, don't you think? Aren't you even curious? She seemed like a wise person," I innocently offered, but Linney looked stunned.

"My mother, wise? No, she was a crazy person. You didn't know her—not like I did. She did hurtful things, like not telling me she was dying."

"That's what I mean, she had her reasons," trying in vain to convince her. "Yes, I guess I didn't know her...not the way you did, but it seemed like she looked out for you." I was realizing Dana knew a lot more than she let on about a lot of things. Linney didn't know Dana the way I did, or that she had looked out for me too.

I feel sad when I remember that we were supposed to meet in a couple of days. I had planned to learn more about her then, but was most looking forward to learning more about myself (everything really).

"What are you talking about?" Linney whines. "She was *not* looking out for me. We never got along, and especially since I came back home!"

"She never mentioned anything about that to me. I heard only good things, maybe a little concern, but... " No, I decide I am finished. I don't want to hear it—Linney's distorted take on things, or think any more about it. I'm not going to convince her. I resent her for being closed off, and for making me feel so protective of Dana and her memory.

I'm blindsided, though, when Linney begs me to go with her to make funeral arrangements. I want to say, "Oh, no, now *you* are the crazy one, not your mother. I couldn't possibly." Instead, I hear myself say, "Okay, if you want me to." I mean, she has no one else.

Somehow, Linney and I manage to get through the funeral arrangements. I am surprised by my own feelings of loss, a sense of the finality of death, and the certainty of my own demise one day, which is not something I had thought too much about before. By the time I get home, I'm exhausted and hungry. I can't eat or sleep though, and stay up until midnight.

I flop on the bed and try to relax, using my remedies and techniques: visualizations, exercises, and all the other things that never work. I end up staring at the ceiling until 3:00 am. Finally, I pick up one of the poetry books scattered at the bottom of my bed. When I feel myself begin to unwind a bit, I "hear" these lines from the last poem I read, like a mantra chanting itself in the dark:

> *That's how you came here, like a star*
> *without a name. Move across the night sky*
> *with those anonymous lights.*

I close my eyes, imagining I am one of those lights —a star moving through the heavens. Instead of the stars living in me, I will live in them. It's the closest I've come to that feeling on the night the stars kept me awake— unguarded—outside the fortress walls.

The memorial service and burial are held on the day Dana and I were supposed to meet, the day I was going to find out everything I always wanted to know, but was afraid to ask. The strange thing is, I slept that night for eight solid hours—the first time in months. I never believed in magic or miracles; now I'm not so sure. Maybe Dana is able to hear all that I was going to ask her, and all that I was going tell her. Maybe my desperation somehow can reach her (wherever she is), and she has pity on me— once again.

For a while I see Linney once or twice a week walking the dog. We wave to each other without a word, but I haven't seen her for a month now. I've called her at least once a week, offering to help with anything she may need.

"Thanks," she always says, "I'm fine. I don't need anything."

"Okay, then. Well, you let me know if you do?" but no word from her—until tonight.

Out of the blue, she calls as I came in the door. She sounds frantic. "You have to come over…*right now!*"

"Okay, be right over," and I break out into a cold sweat at the prospect of what I will find, what I will see or hear.

The sun is going down. It's dark and icy cold. The ocean is roaring, maybe churning up for a Nor'easter. I walk over to Dana's house and go in through the kitchen door—the one I wandered into the night of the sleeping pill fiasco.

Dana's house always looked staged for a photo shoot. On her tables and shelves, here and there, she would place bluebells in the spring, seashells and feathers in the summer, autumn leaves in the fall, moss and crystals in winter. I liked the displays of seasonal warmth, light and color, but now it looks more like my place, not at all inviting—no frills, dark, and kind of messy. I notice flower arrangements left from the funeral on the countertop and kitchen table, wilted and dried.

"In here," Linney calls from the small office off of the kitchen, lamplight spilling over the doorway. The room is as if Dana has just walked out of it, and will be "back in a sec," as she would say. It is now, I guess, the single welcoming, orderly and bright spot in the entire house.

Looking up, Linney says, "I *made* myself come in here early this morning." I assume she has been in here all day.

"Oh, how? I mean ... you said you never wanted to ..." She cuts me off, running her hand through her long hair in a nervous gesture.

"I know…I know. I never wanted to come in here, but I…I had this dream last night. My mom was calling me, but I couldn't find her. I wandered through the rooms, but it was kinda like I was outside too, trying to get in. You know how dreams are weird like that? The wind kept pushing me back. I could see inside the house. Waves were crashing against the windows from the inside, and I heard the wind howling and…roaring, sounding like a train coming. It woke me up.

"It was still dark, but I could see the light coming from the lamp in the office. It hasn't been on since Mom died. I thought maybe *she* made it come on, like…her way of calling me in here. I feel like I'm still in a dream now, or," Linney hesitates, "or awake for the first time—not sure which."

Me too!

I brace myself when she says that, but I can't say a word. I notice Linney looks different tonight, still sad, but softer, more composed, and somehow, yes, more "awake." The glow in the room illuminates her long hair, and the gold trim at the collar and cuffs of her nightshirt. I keep my gaze on her and try to focus as she begins to show me some of the things Dana left for her. She opens a picture album.

"These are pictures of us, of me, when I was a little, when Dad was still alive." She points to a photo of herself in a pine tree, taken from the ground up. The branches look like a feathery green staircase with Linney looking down and waving. There is another of Dana holding a little Linney up with one hand under a white beach umbrella dotted with blue fish.

"I didn't know. I didn't know...so many things," she whispers, as if I am not even here. She picks up a worn, white journal, and holds it close to her. "I didn't know Mom wrote in this when I was growing up."

"Maybe you didn't need to know...until now."

Pictures and papers are strewn over the desk, and in its open drawers. She picks up a page, "I've been reading this letter over and over." She doesn't read it out loud to me, but I sense it must have broken a silence, opened a door or shattered some walls. Maybe filled a void?

Linney opens another small book with a black leather cover embossed with tiny white stars. She turns the pages, pausing to read some of Dana's entries, her fingers tracing along the lines. On the first page is the date of Dana's diagnosis, a description of her treatment plan, and her intention to keep her illness from Linney, apparently also her thoughts and feelings through it all. Linney reads lines from poems on virtues that meant something to Dana:

On hope as, "a thing with feathers/that perches on the soul," and on faith, like the moon, "faithful, even as it fades from fullness/slowly becoming that last curving and impossible/sliver of light before the final darkness." Dana mentions a "year of miracles," gratitude and joy through her last days spent with her daughter at home, but also of her companion, "constant sorrow."

I am feeling like Dana left these treasures for me too when Linney asks me to read the last entries. I am lightheaded and disoriented as I read what Dana wrote in her graceful handwriting, my voice barely audible, far away sounding, like it is not me speaking:

> *Pain — has an Element of Blank —*
> *It cannot recollect*
> *When it began — or if there were*
> *A time when it was not —*

And

> *The Heart asks Pleasure–first–*
> *And then–Excuse from Pain–*
> *And then–those little Anodynes*
> *That deaden suffering–*
>
> *And then–to go to sleep–*
> *And then–if it should be*
> *The will of its Inquisitor*
> *The liberty to die–*

I look up at Linney, tears in her eyes, holding a small package wrapped in dark blue tissue, bound with silver ribbon.

"She left this for you. Open it. I want to see."

"Really?" I take it into my trembling hands and unwrap it.

It is a book of poetry by Emily Dickinson with a note:

For Stella,
With Hope and Faith
From Dana

Outside the night is still and silent, no stars, and sea fog is drifting in.

True Minds

Of a husband, enduring memories of all that is lost to him

He presses his forehead against the cold window pane until it fogs over. The front and back doors are locked, and his keys do not open them. At the side of the cottage, he separates the thick growth of vines and peers into the bedroom window. Nothing remains of what had been in place when he left that morning.

He feels himself telescoping to a distance above, looking down on the scene, watching himself wander back to the front yard. Next to the bare willow tree he sees the sign: FOR SALE.

He heads for the pub in town.

Inside, the warmth and dim lights are a familiar welcome. It's a busy Friday night, with only a few seats left at the bar. The sounds of end-of-week chatter fill the space. He sits furthest from the door, the wind rushing in, with wet snowflakes and the last of the autumn leaves. Avoiding the mirror behind the bar, he fixes his eyes on the array of bottles in various shapes and colors below it. He tries not to, but can't help thinking about those early years when they came here together every Friday night, taking one of those cozy side tables, where other young couples are seated now, clinking glasses, smiling, their lives ahead of them.

He is remembering how they each would order a different cocktail of creamy pink, frothy green, sweet and fruity or the "grown up" ones—clear, amber-colored and bitter. It was all amusement, sipping from the other's glass. He does not care to recall how many years it has been since he began coming here alone—first at lunchtime, then most nights.

He tries to lose himself in the music, the noise, the vodka, forget for now that she is gone, and all that is lost to him. After a second double vodka, his mind and memory cloud over, and his heart is a cold stone.

He drinks until the bartender leans into him, "Better get going." This time, he gets up without protest, and sets his course for the few blocks back to the vacant building he used to call home. *Home, home, home* swirls in his mind like the frozen flakes sweeping around him.

He has already decided, he will stay the night in the empty house. When he arrives, he stares at the little cottage, trying to bring it into focus, remembering the sounds and warmth of it when he arrived, unsuspecting, the night before. Unsteady, he manages to make his way to his car to get the blanket—the one that's been in the back seat since the children were small. He crunches over the frozen walkway to the back door, covers his fist with the blanket and shatters the window. He pulls out a few shards of glass, and edges his hand in to unlock the door.

He turns up the heat to warm the icy cold, and stumbles into the bedroom they once had called "the marriage suite." He wraps himself in the meager blanket printed with elephants and balloons, and falls to the floor.

After a sound sleep, he opens his eyes to morning light, feeling wide awake, despite a headache. The memories and self-reproach he warded off the night before flood in with a brilliance, like the sun shafts on the bare wall in front of him. He pads to the bathroom to splash his face. He notices pieces of the white shaving mug with blue sailboats—shattered on the floor—in nowise reparable.

He wants to make himself presentable, make a plan, make some calls, get everything straightened out once and for all. Instead, he returns to the bleak room, eases himself down to the floor and stares at the ceiling, where memories begin to appear as visions before him, some bitter and dark, some too sweet and too light to bear.

THE MEETING

She was lovely, vibrant, open and gentle—and as lonely as he, both of them ambitious with the necessary, youthful illusions about life, love and themselves. They grew up in the small, seacoast town in New England, but hadn't traveled in the same social circles. She went to private high school off the island; he had thought her snobby. He was a star soccer player at the public high school; she thought him arrogant. They had mutual friends, but not until they were home on spring break in their last year of college did they really "see" each other.

That summer arrived with promise in the air and wonder in each other, in the place they had lived all their lives, discovering it together as a new world The woods they had walked in as children were now, Arden forest itself," she had said. They whiled away the days on warm beaches, chatted on sunny cafe decks, shared oysters and champagne at intimate tables overlooking the bay, and hiked on rocky paths high above the ocean.

In the evening lying together, ocean air wafting in and the light and color of sunset filling her small room, she read sonnets to him and said, "I feel I am in a Matisse painting." He could not stop wondering if her interest in him would fade in the fall. Their first Christmas together, she gave him a self portrait she had attempted, reminiscent of Matisse. He copied lines from a sonnet she had once read to him:

> *Love alters not with his brief hours and weeks,*
> *But bears it out even to the edge of doom.*

He rolled the parchment into a scroll, placed it in a tiny bottle and tucked it into a small boat he had carved out of driftwood.

He adored her for challenging him to think beyond their place and time; she loved that he urged her to be in the here and now, the simplicity of which she respected and felt was true. In short, each had sensibilities and qualities the other lacked; they felt a void being filled, a missing piece fitting into place to make a whole of their life puzzles.

One day they sat resting along Old Garden Path, he looking out across the rocky cliffs that dropping off from a height to small slivers of seaweed-strewn strands. She was reading Albert Camus and often felt anxiety setting in at what she found in his existentialist musings, but also understood much of it as plain common sense.

"Listen to this. Camus says a person should know about himself," she read, 'like the palm of his hand, know the exact number of his defects…know how far he can go, foretell his failures…and, above all, accept these things.'"

He remained gazing out to sea until she asked, "Well, what do you think?"

"What's the point? I think it's impossible," putting his arm around her, "but I guess we still have a few years to figure it out—if that's the goal, but I don't want to try to foretell my failures, whatever that means. I'd rather move toward my successes, wouldn't you?"

"Well, yeah, sure, but if we don't get some perspective now, I mean…"

"Oh, look, something out there just beyond the waves," spotting a form bobbing and turning above the surface. They began running, keeping their eyes on the figure appearing and disappearing again into the blue-green waves. Further out, white sails drifted all in a row.

"A whale?"

"A seal?"

Then they lost sight of the shiny sleek form in the sun reflecting off the water. Overheated and exhausted, they dropped to the ground, laughing and holding each other.

❧

He hears it now—her summer laugh, long since silenced. By the new year, they had planned on marrying one day and settling near that path with a view of sea meeting sky. But not until establishing careers in Boston—law for him, journalism for her. Many plans came into focus, but they married earlier than they had planned—with a child on the way. Then those plans were stretched out over many years until they vanished into a distant horizon.

He turns his eyes away from the ceiling, closes them for a moment and sits up. The sun has moved across the room. He wants to get up, but, he lies down again to see what else will be revealed to him, as if he has no control over the apparitions.

THE MARRIAGE

There she is—so young, fresh, beautiful. He can smell her scent; feel her softness, hear her voice, see her gestures—light and fine. It is pain to recall his urgent desire, fierce and fiery and later, his resentment that she had neither his intense, frequent appetite, nor his need for intimacy.

Then come images of the cottage passed on to her from an aunt who had stipulated that it be in her niece's name only, warning that, "Mr Right was all wrong." His senses fill with sights and sounds of how it once had been: manicured lawn, hydrangeas and lilacs; children playing under the willow tree, white sheets billowing out from the clothesline like sails in the wind. He thinks of the salty scent of them tucked into the bed. They had brought their babies home and lay with them there, she nursing and singing them to sleep, he yet unaware of life changing—slowly, but already shifting.

With free-lance writing and waitressing at the pub, she supported him through law school. He didn't find a "suitable" Boston law firm, insisting on a practice in town, "safer and close to home."

"The worst decision of your life and a curse ever after on you, our family and the town," she later railed. For her, securing work, care of the children, private school tuitions, domestic chores, all came before him, he knew. Years expanded into decades, her intended brilliant career seemingly impossible, or so she thought, with children and responsibilities, and his practice languishing in lethargy amid town talk of questionable dealing and compromises.

As the past spreads out before him, even now, he feels the old desire—despite the years of refusals and excuses, she merely tolerating his lips, his hands, his weight, with the knowledge that she knew that he knew.

The vivid colors of their dreams faded; neither having measured up to the expectations of the other, or of themselves.

❧

A SHATTERED VESSEL

It all came with a searing clarity one night, on a business trip in San Francisco where he visited an old friend, recently remarried. The couple couldn't wait to show him the courtyard they had designed and created together. It was edged with lush ferns in front of fragrant, night-blooming jasmine, its white blossoms wavering like sparks in the moonlight. He noted how kindly they spoke to each other, how he deferred to her, how she looked at him, how they finished each other's thoughts, and held hands after dinner.

On the way to his room that evening, he caught sight of them through their half-opened door. In gentle embrace, they leaned into each other, gestures full of promise. He closed the door behind him and stood by the window, unable to move, a warm breeze drifting in off the bay. The light and weight of the evening was a revelation to him, but also an irrevocable blow.

That night he dreamed his wife came to him in the dark. When she drew near in a white flowing robe, he saw it was all jasmine flowers. He inhaled the fragrance of their perfume. When he reached for her, she vanished, and he awakened. He intended to stay awake, review his life, put it into perspective, but he fell back to sleep.

When he arrived home the next day, he seemed to notice for the first time that the cottage was in sore need: rotting cedar shakes, cracked chimney, leaning picket fence, crumbing stone wall and unweeded gardens. Likewise, his office now seemed dark, damp and cluttered. He allowed himself to recall the old rumors about his practice and his marriage. He sensed how things were and were not, but didn't know what to do. He came to believe there was nothing to be done. He did nothing.

Again, he rolls over, props himself up, wanting to leave that house, but once more he gives over to the last scenes playing out in between futile questions:
What if I had? Why didn't I? If only I could have.

&

THE IMPEDIMENTS

It had been a long decline: the practice, the cottage, the marriage, he begging her to love him, she begging him to save his reputation and their family. He feels the sting of harsh, accusatory words exchanged one too many times and imprinted on the other's soul. They seemed now to reverberate in the empty room.

They had once been pure vessels waiting to be filled to the brim with all that was lacking, wishing to be known by the other, to learn from the other what yet was unknown. What each needed was taken in at first, a thirst quenched, and savored. With time, the other's deficits were exposed, and the draft grew bitter with resentment.

Don't see me as I am. Don't change me.

How many lovers discover that neither one receives what is longed for, what they think they want, need or deserve? To be free to develop separately, yet to live and grow together. How? Maybe that wisdom can be imparted in an instant, or take a lifetime, if ever. Lovers' illusions and self-deceptions, unfounded rationales, too much pain and sore need, all intertwined.

Infinite are the ways of creating a glittering shell of appearance, while the core of suffering goes unseen, unnoticed, unacknowledged. What devices, defenses and denials mask the myriad roots reaching in every direction, compromising a once solid structure?

Quiet, quiet...hear the vines growing?

❧

With daylight already fading, he lifts himself up. He runs his fingers through his hair and wraps the blanket around his shoulders. He goes to pick up the pieces of the shattered mug and puts them in his pocket. He wanders into each room, lingering a moment, then goes through to the kitchen. He covers the broken window with the blanket. Next to the magnet on the refrigerator: "If you're going through hell, keep going," he leaves a note:

I am a wandering bark.

Outside, the day's sun has melted last night's snow. Rivulets run through the cracks in the walkway. He pulls at a strand of ivy clinging to the cottage wall until it loosens and carries it with him to the pub.

Cruel Sunset
Of a woman whose universe collapses

Over the hills the sunset is cruel—a dull glow through low clouds—not the perfect ending to this day. If it were perfect, the sun would be flaming orange, a haughty disc, descending nobility above the crowd of tree tops struck golden with its rays. The sky would be a cloudless blue and brilliant, like the light-filled thoughts that had crystallized for her not long ago. Still, she feels perfect contentment, the lush spring grass at her feet, crammed with violets.

"I have always loved you."

Was it only this morning she quit her job, left her lover, grew wings? It seems ages ago now, with remembrance of herself then—another being, in another universe, chanting a mock litany walking to her car after work each day: "unholy ones, speakers of lies, self-deceivers, clueless children of darkness." She had never believed it was in her nature to have such thoughts, to assign derisive names to others, or to just walk away—as she had today.

She no longer lives in that universe. It began falling in on itself the night the rains came, transforming her world, unraveling it into wider and wider spirals, outward to infinite nothingness, or whatever universes do when they expand then collapse. It was a way to imagine and understand it all.

When she left her father not more than a month ago, he was breathing heavily, his eyes closed, his hands restless, his fingers moving rhythmically in strange gestures. Those movements and murmurings were as if from some arcane ritual. She sang to him, read to him, recited poetry, though she knew he couldn't hear her, at least not in the usual way.

When she spoke the line, "I will arise and go now," he moaned and lifted his head.

The next day, after some hours of quiet struggle, he died. She had not been able to bring herself to hold his hand, or rest her head on his shoulder, as did her sister. Instead, she remained at the foot of his bed all the while, not fully present in the solemnity of death, with dullness of mind and numbness of soul. As his breathing got quieter, his face paled and went grey like a sad sky. Then his eyes opened wide and gazed up to the right, as if looking at whomever he had been communicating with the night before—his mother, his wife, his son—all gone before him.

She didn't believe, though she wanted to, that in an afterlife souls reunite with loved ones gone before. Did she even want to be with anyone she had known in this life, after she herself crossed over to another world, if there is another? It wasn't that she hadn't cared about her family, yet she had resentment, remorse, regret, and there was love too—all mixed together.

Still, she sometimes wondered if, in a dream-like state, souls recognize each other's higher self—the one they may have only sensed or glimpsed in life. Do they agree to come back together over many lifetimes in various constellations of relationship to live out the karma they themselves create—little universes coming into being and dissolving over and over, until all manner of things shall be well?

She was only sixteen when it was arranged for her child to be given up. She thought she had accepted the why and wherefore of it. What else could she do, her life ahead of her, and having brought shame upon herself and her family? Back then, it had not occurred to her that there was *only* blame, no comfort offered, no empathy expressed, no emotional preparation to cope with the thing she had to do. How could she have known what it would mean to live in the silence of sorrow and bitter shame ever after, to have the memory of going into labor, not knowing what to expect?

She had asked her father, "Do you still love me?"

"Let's just get this thing over with," his response.

How could she have known what it would mean to be anesthetized at the sacred moment of birth, so she could not remember it; what it would mean to relive the burning memory of having looked into the eyes of forever as she handed over a tiny being to a stranger—to she knew not what? And the reverberating in her heart of a silent goodbye to flesh of her flesh—a green and tender limb torn from a living tree.

Time passes; life goes on, doesn't it?

The father of her child went off to college, and they drifted apart. And so she was alone in the evening to weep into her pillow so as not to be heard—a cruel and unusual punishment to have been a young girl grieving, with small hands pressing on her heart in the dark, until they pressed in so far, she couldn't feel anything.

Until the night the rains came.

Then all through those nights she listens for what could have been heard, hears what *should* have been said, and all that could have been forgiven—or not. She recalls the hours before her father's death—how her sister closed the dead man's eyes, the pain of a lost child, and the years of silent grief. Day and night her mind wide open overflows and drifts in worlds of love and loss, in her futile wish to be cherished by her lover—enough to leave his wife—a promise made so many times. The sound of rain pounding through the cold silence from long ago found a home in her heart, a feeling in the blood of each beat, awakening with clarity all that had been, and all that had not.

Out of death-piercing loss and yearning, she opens to everything rising before her in the dark, breaking the silence, formulating the questions, speaking them out loud, penetrating through to the hard-shelled seed in her heart, with no way to sprout or blossom.

During the weeks of the rain, she is changing, how she doesn't know, into another, truer form of herself. Without sinking to the depths, how can one rise to the surface? A cold heart is warming; the hard shell watered with tears is opening. A bud is forming, burgeoning to blossom into the balm of compassion—for the love that remains, which can never be given to the lost child, but to the young girl she had been, and the woman she has become.

Then, one morning she awakens to quiet, in the golden light of a May sunrise. She feels clean and bright—her senses cleared—a hard-won knowledge grasped in an awareness of all that was and all that wasn't, the irreconcilable past separated from what is possible and awaiting. She thinks of the wisdom she had heard so often, but never understood how to live it:

To every thing there is a season, and a time to every purpose under the heaven....A time to be born, and a time to die ....a time to break down, and a time to build up....A time to weep, and a time to laugh; a time to mourn and a time to dance ....A time to cast away stones, and a time to gather stones together....a time to keep silence, and a time to speak.

She knows what she must do to redeem her former self and to emerge into what had yet to be created.

No one notices when she comes into work late, or that she is a different being from the one they think they know. No one except her boss, her lover, who meets the newly-hatched being without feathers. She will no longer remain in a dead-end job and relationship, and intends to live more in freedom than dependency, more in joy than sadness.

She flies into his office to tell him she will not see him this Wednesday, or any other Wednesday, not ever again. "Please pick up your things on the front walk of the apartment—today," with pleasure in the thought of his taking away the few things he had given her over the years, along with an unkept promise.

Let him take them back to that house I had so often driven past on the other nights of the week to gaze at the warm light shining through the windows, imaging the lives lived within— apart from mine.

She tells him that she knows that he knows she had kept his company from going under time and again.

Was that the reason he granted me one night a week—as recompense instead of a raise, or a kept promise?

"I will no longer be here to cover your inadequacies and inabilities, financial and otherwise," were her last words to a story she could not have dreamed a short time ago would end with such a sense of satisfaction.

On this new day, she returns home, makes French toast and coffee, goes into town to buy a new white coverlet and two bright printed pillows for her bed, walks on a wooded path, picks purple and white wild flowers, has dinner at her favorite restaurant, content to be alone and free.

Walking home on a trail by the river, she sees geese gathering on the still water and watches as they wheel up into the grey sky in clamorous farewell. And there, on the horizon, she observes the imperfect sunset.

It comes to her that the litany of names she used to assign to others were really names she could have called herself—the self she used to be—light years ago, before she told the violets she loved them.

Now she imagines herself a deity preparing to assign true names to all things in her new universe.

Shiva's Table
Of a young actress who deludes herself

She turns her head as the sound of gentle rain becomes a pelting sleet against the window behind her. Weary and chilled, she pulls a wooly throw over her, only her two hands uncovered to hold a bag of chips and a Coke bottle. She settles on the sofa to watch a new show everyone at work had been talking about, *Living and Loving in Brooklyn*. She wonders what is meant by "living."

The TV screen flashes psychedelic colors and patterns. The five-minutes of pre-show commercials blare out for Viagra, Volkswagen and Kraft macaroni and cheese.

"Good combination," she blurts out.

The first scene opens on a lovely courtyard: a beautiful, slim young woman sitting at a table with her morning coffee. Picture perfect. Something drops from above, past the branch of a tree, as her eyes follow it to the ground.

"A condom!" she shrieks.

Another perfect female opens a French door, peeks out, glancing with a slight grimace at its landing place, as if it were an everyday occurrence. The women begin jabbering about work: waiting on tables and hedge funds. The subject turns to men, their upcoming dates that night and lingerie, with allusions to *Fifty Shades of Grey*.

"This is crap."

Reaching for the remote, she surfs through the channels: pawn shop dealers, rattlesnake hunters, political analysis, and cooking competitions. She throws it across the room, disgusted at the taste of "some people," but more so at her having finished off all the chips and half a liter of Coke. Licking the salt around her lips, she drops the chip bag to the floor and places the Coke bottle next to it. She passes her hand over the little roll of flesh above the waist of her pajama bottoms, "Oh, God!"

She stretches her hand to the side table, grabs her reading glasses and places them on the tip of her nose. She picks up *Love on the Subway* beside her, which she has been trying to get through since last spring. After reading the same page twice, she slams it shut and throws it to the floor.

"This is crap, too." Leaping up from the sofa, she tips over the vase of holly she had placed there yesterday for a little "holiday spirit," knocking over the Coke bottle. Picking up the book, the chip bag, the vase and bottle, she stomps to the kitchen and tosses them in the trash. Returning to clean up the spill, she pricks her finger on a holly leaf.

"What the hell?"

Though she had held it in all day, now it bursts through, her breath coming in short gasps. As if in a fog, through misty eyes, she picks up the phone.

"Hey, it's me, Jessica," her strained voice near hysteria, her mind wavering between thoughts of what she had hoped and wished for, and the grim reality she now has to bear. Between sobs and stammers, she speaks of dark revelations of the morning and her confession of self-loathing, guilt and shame.

"I'll be right over...hold on," comes the familiar voice with an Italian accent.

❧

Two winters ago, Jessica had escaped from a dreary town in Ohio to bustling Brooklyn. Her life is not as she had imagined when she first arrived.

"I'm here," she had reassured her mother. "I'm good, Ma. It's gonna be alright, so don't worry." She wanted to believe it herself, and it was—at first. "I met everyone at The Studio today. I've gotta do this," not wanting to return a failure to that wretched town.

Acting was her dream, her reason for being, or so she believed. Accepted to study at The Studio, a well-known and respected theatre company, and having found work as a hostess at a popular corner bistro a few blocks away, her new life had almost begun.

The few things she had brought with her to New York she had carefully positioned around the small ground floor apartment: a French nightstand under the window facing the alley; a white cushioned chair in the corner near an exposed brick wall; an ornate, black metal floor lamp with a bright yellow shade next to the faux fireplace. Near the sliding door to a small patio, she placed a wicker stand holding a dark-leafed plant dotted with tiny pink flowers, which bloomed through the winter, how she didn't know. The small, red side-table awaited an affordable sofa to be placed against the wall facing the fireplace. She felt ecstatic whenever she could afford to add something new and needed.

Her favorite find was spotted among props being discarded at The Studio to make room for recent, more desirable donations. She rescued the round, glass-top table with bronze legs in the shape of tree branches. Months later, after searching everywhere, she still hadn't sat at it, not having found the "just right" chairs to compliment it.

Then, walking from the bus stop one breezy spring evening, the fragrance of lilac in the air, she noticed two chairs placed one on top of the other under a blossoming cherry tree. As she picked them up, she noticed across the street, a striking, dark-haired man leaning against a porch post watching her intently. In the raking light cast by late afternoon sun, his white shirt was bright against his face and hair. When she saw him, she waved, feeling a little embarrassed to be seen awkwardly hauling the sidewalk finds. He did not wave back, but kept his gaze on her.

His image remained with her as she made her way home—those piercing eyes seemingly looking through her. As she cleaned the chairs that evening, she wondered about the stranger, and had already decided to walk that way again soon.

Oh, how lovely, she marveled at her good fortune

when she noticed the metal work on the backs of the chairs was in a vine and leaf design, like the table's legs. One was brushed in places with silver leaf and the other with gold leaf. "There, now," she sighed, with an extraordinary sense of satisfaction. The chairs had found a home across from each other at the little table that had stood alone for so long. She felt that it meant something, maybe that she was settled at last, and that more good things were in store for her.

She had planned to make a cup of tea, sit at the table for the first time, and finish reading *The Merchant of Venice*, as she was determined to read all of Shakespeare's plays in her new life, but a drowsiness came on suddenly. Feeling drained, she went straight to bed.

That night she dreamed she was sitting at the table. The windows above it open, the wind howling, and the driving rain coming in. The front door blew open, and the dark-haired man entered and came to sit across from her at the table. They looked into each others' eyes in silence. His were deep, dark and penetrating, expressing a longing, like her own yearning for love and intimacy.

When she awoke, she did not remember having gone to bed the night before. She felt a little unsteady as she walked over to open the bedroom door and peeked out, half expecting to find the dark man at the table waiting for her. Her sleepiness faded, but all through the day, the vivid dream did not.

Was there some hidden message or portent in the dream?

On her way home from The Studio that evening, she felt compelled to walk past the house where she had seen the mystery man. She knew dreams could feel so real, their images lingering, but usually fade and are forgotten in time. The dream did not fade, but remained with her—day and night. She began walking home that way at least once a week, certain that the dream *did* mean something.

A whole scenario formed, as she fantasized that she would see him again, be with him, make love, marry him, have his child. Sometimes she had to stop herself, *No, no, no, no...this is not why I came here. What is wrong with me?* She had no answer, but could not shake off the day dreaming and her unbidden desires.

When the weather began to turn cold, she walked the shorter way home, avoiding that street, that house, and the mysterious man who wasn't there. Yet, wasn't everything in her life now on the upswing? At the bistro, the manager, who had a nickname for everyone, called her aside.

"Hey, J Lo, you gotta way aboutcha, and customahs love ya." He gave her a raise and a few more hours a week.

With the extra money, she was able to further adorn her living space with a sofa, a bright Tibetan carpet and framed photos of Cobble Hill, the Brooklyn Bridge and Coney Island. She also bought several figures of Hindu gods and goddesses and placed them where they could "watch over her," or so she liked to believe. Shiva, dancing in a ring of fire, held pride of place on the half shelf above the front door.

She now had a circle of fellow actors who met weekly at a tavern in the Village. Her life was falling into place, but still with a sense that there was much more to come. She attributed every good fortune and coincidence to the dream, the dark-haired man and his "presence" in her life.

Less than a month after she had randomly decided to read *The Merchant of Venice*, there was an open audition call posted for it at The Studio—an upcoming off, off Broadway production. With the encouragement of one of her instructors and several friends, she prepared and went to the audition. Weeks later, after having given up on hearing, she got a call back and was offered the leading role of Portia. She felt it had nothing to do with her talent.

It was destiny.

The good news spread, and a friend put her in touch with Gena, a more experienced actor, who also had landed a part in the play. They arranged to meet for coffee and immediately clicked, though they were nothing alike. Gena was laid back and laughed at everything.

"Isn't it funny. I got the part of Jessica, and you're Jessica in real life?"

Jessica, more serious and cynical, thought, *whatever real life is.* "Yeah, ironic...hey, did you get the invitation to the director's pre-rehearsal party?"

Gena laughed the answer to Jessica's question,"Yes, I did. I am so excited about it. Why don't we go together? Can't wait to meet the director. Don't know him; hope he's not a tyrant."

"Sure, let's go together, why not? I don't think he'll be a tyrant...not sure why, but... "

"Great, let's do it. What are you going to wear?" Gena wanted to know, while Jessica fell into a dream.

From the moment Jessica got the part, she imagined the play's director, Leon Lorenzo *was* the dark-haired man who had arranged everything exactly as it was happening and would happen—world without end, amen. She asked around, and searched everywhere for an image of him, his address or any personal information, but found nothing to connect him with her imagined paramour.

She took to reaching up to touch the little golden figure of Shiva above the doorway whenever she left or entered her apartment, like a ritual blessing with holy water at a church door. She would remain on the threshold for a few seconds to remind herself she was on the brink of ... something.

All of her free time was devoted to memorizing Portia's lines, reciting them in the shower; during lulls at the bistro; in elevators; on the subway and late into the night. Anticipating, yet apprehensive about going to the director's party, she began to methodically plan what she would wear, how she would smile, what she would say—when at last she would meet him face to face—her mentor, her lover, her all. She lost five pounds, splurged on a short black dress with tiny silver sparkles in a small swirl around one shoulder, and black boots with grey patent leather dots around the top—perfect.

When the night of the director's rehearsal party arrived, she spent hours at the mirror, applying make-up which she usually did not wear. She straightened and arranged her hair, which she usually left frizzled. All the while, the practical part of her knew she was out of control. The director was *not, could not* be, the dark-haired man. But the deepest part of her did not believe the other part.

Ready or not, here I go.

Wrapped in a magenta mohair shawl, She reaches above the door to touch Shiva, standing perfectly still for a moment, her eyes closed. Then she is out to meet Gena at the subway station.

There's Gena, waving crazily as Jessica approached, waving back and picking up her pace. Gena is a vision in white leggings, pale blue silk Indian tunic; blue and white veil over her head, embroidered with darker blue, silver and white filigree designs.

The street light shone behind her like a halo, as snow flurries drifting around her.

Gena looks like the Virgin Mary.

"Mother of God, it's cold!" Jessica shouted, as she hurried toward Gena.

"You look heavenly."

"Thanks, Jess. You too, bee-oo-tee-ful."

"Neither one of us is dressed for this weather though," Jessica said through chattering teeth. Joining arms, they stepped onto the escalator and down into the depths of the city.

After manic small talk, alternate expressions of anxiety and humor, they arrived at the Upper East Side apartment building. Dreading to be the earliest, overly eager guests, the women went around the block in the frigid air, laughing in giddy anticipation, then came back to squeeze into the small foyer and pressed the nose of a brass gargoyle bell.

In the elevator, Jessica felt a gurgling in her lower abdomen. When she caught sight of herself in the mirrored walls, she didn't recognize her reflection. Whatever confidence she had earlier dwindled into self-consciousness.

I'm overdressed. I look ridiculous. Even Gena looks better; at least her appearance has conversational value. What am I doing here, anyway? How did I get this part? I want to go home.

And she didn't mean to Brooklyn.

When the elevator doors opened, the women turned left, but hearing voices and music spilling out into the hall in the other direction, they backtracked to the door opened to a candle-lit room. They stepped in, unnoticed at first, making their way amidst small groups of the guests, some looking as put together as Jessica had hoped to be. Others were in jeans and tee shirts, and plenty others outfitted for at least as much conversational mileage as Gena's "get up" had.

Everyone stood mingling, smiling with drinks in hand. When she was spotted by a few of her Studio friends, who pointed and brought attention to her as Portia, others gathered around to introduce themselves, offer congratulations and ask questions.

A glass of wine was put into her hand by a short man with penetrating green eyes, flowing white hair and charming Italian accent. He called her Portia, identifying himself as Shylock. He put his arm through hers and led her across the room to meet the other cast members, but she was distracted, looking past shoulders and heads, scanning the room for that one face and those eyes.

All the while, he talked non-stop of the theory of Shakespeare not being the author of the plays, interpretations of *The Merchant of Venice*, and the upcoming rehearsals.

Jessica began to sense "Shylock" was scrutinizing her—reading her thoughts, intuiting her wild expectations —all crunching against one another into the fantasy of what she wished for, not what she knew to be true, yet she could not bring herself back from her habitual, frenzied imaginings.

"I will fetch you another glass of the excellent Pouilly Fuisse, no?"

"The what? Oh, yes, thank you," though she was already feeling a bit tipsy.

She continued to search the room, anxious and disheartened. When Shylock returned, she blurted out, "Where's Leon, the director? You'd think he'd have the *courtesy* to appear and introduce himself by now, don't you?"

"My dear, Portia, the merciless, *I* am Leon; I thought you knew."

Handing her the wine glass, he clinked his to hers, "Chin-chin." Then he took a small silver spoon out of the breast pocket of his black velvet vest and tapped it on his glass to call the room to whatever order was possible. He welcomed everyone, made announcements about the rehearsal schedules and handed out play books.

Jessica stood in a daze. For her, the rest of the evening blurred, her foolish hopes crushed. On the way home, she said nothing in response to Gena's constant chatter, seething with resentment that Shylock, the director, unbeknownst to him and unintended, had already exacted his pound of flesh.

That was six months ago. Now, on this evening, she tries to calm herself waiting for Leon to arrive to confess her obsession with the dark man, her illusions about how she thought her life would be, and the dreadful revelations of that morning.

Since her starring role in *The Merchant of Venice*, she had no callbacks, even though the play had a successful run, and she had received rave reviews. She had gone to very few auditions, despite encouragement and references from Leon. Her group of friends had fallen away one by one.

Have I isolated myself from them…from everything?

"Hey, business ain't what it use ta be, J Lo," her boss had called to tell her that her hours had to be cut back.

Maybe my turning up late and calling in sick too often is the real reason? Maybe acting was not the reason I came here. Now this!

She had long wanted to tell Leon, to whom she had grown close during the run of the play, of her secret and crazy imaginings, but never had. Now, she waits at the door to hear his footsteps. The sleet has turned to snow, dropping lightly to the earth below and falling against the window pane. She stares at the blank TV screen, waiting, waiting, always waiting.

There, oh, there he is.

She pulls open the door before Leon can knock and reaches for him, inhaling the cold of the icy flakes on his jacket.

"Shhh, now…shhh," he whispers to her as she rests her head on his shoulder. Leon strokes her hair,

"Now, come, sit with me."

Jessica holds on to him as they walk to the forsaken table, where she sits for the first time across from him, he on the silver chair, she on the gold. She tells him of her obsession with the dark mystery man, her imaginary savior, and of the morning's grim discovery.

She recounts how the night before she had walked on the street where she had first seen him—having become almost a sacred ritual. From across the way, she looked to the house where the dark-haired man had stood watching her that spring evening.

"There was yellow tape stretched around the sidewalk and porch. When I saw that, I thought someone must have hurt him…or killed him. I rushed home to see if there was any news on the TV or radio, but there was nothing. I left the radio on all night…almost a sleepless one, waiting to hear about…of a tragedy…anything about the house or person in it. Then, this morning I tried to make sense of what I was hearing on the breaking news. There *was* a victim—a boy, and a suspect—a man."

She tells Leon, now completely shaken and in tears, how she rushed to see on the news her dream of the dark-haired man turn to nightmare. She watched as he was taken out of that house in handcuffs. He was *not* the victim as she had feared, but a perpetrator, not an inscrutable lover, but a predator who had kidnapped a young boy, kept him in a cage and abused him for over a year.

Leon takes Jessica's hands in his, having heard of the tragedies of the shattered fantasy, and fate of an innocent child.

"Oh, Leon, I'm so ashamed, what a crazy, selfish... that boy...that poor child. Maybe I could have done something...anything. And I...I..."

"My dear, Jessica," Leon sighs, "it is you who must now have mercy on *yourself*. You could not have known... or done anything. How...how?"

"But, I..."

"When illusions end, Cara mia, life can begin," taking her hand.

They sit in silence looking into each other's eyes, at the once lonely table, she contemplating the destruction of a foolish dream, and imagining the creation of a new reality.

From time to time, she casts her gaze to Shiva dancing in a ring of fire.

A Matter of Time
Of a therapist who loved a saint

He had given away every last penny of an enormous inheritance. He was homeless now, but it didn't matter, only he missed being able to help others. I found this out when a stranger called me and told me Kenny had given him fifteen-hundred dollars to see me for as many therapy sessions as that amount would cover. Inheriting a fortune is everyone's ultimate fantasy, but Kenny just handed his out like cupcakes at a birthday party.

So, Kenny must have gotten a windfall from his Aunt Molly who, as I remember, had no other family. I met her when we stayed at her place on Martha's Vineyard. And what a place it was. I guess he gave that away too.

"Wait, now let me get this straight," I said to the caller. "Kenny is broke and homeless, and you are using his last fifteen hundred dollars to get help from me?"

"Oh, well, yeah…I guess. I mean, he said you'd be able ta help me. I wasn't sleepin' nights since my dad died and all, and a lot a other things happened too—lost my job, that kinda thing. Kenny said you'd help me, and I believe 'im. He gave me the money before he was homeless though."

"Well, that makes all the difference," I said, trying not to laugh, or cry. I felt bad, being sarcastic like that, but I don't think he noticed.

"Let's see what I've got here on my calendar. Next Tuesday at 2:00 pm, is that good for you?"

"Sure thing, Doc, see ya then."

I jotted down his contact info. "Okay, see you next week."

Kenny, homeless? That was hard to take. I was sorry I hadn't asked some of the questions I was formulating in those few minutes on the phone—some I had since I'd last seen Kenny. I knew it would be wrong, asking my questions of a new client in a first session. He was the one looking for answers, but I figured I would get at least some answers over time—that is, if he even showed up.

Not that I didn't want to help the caller—Sam was his name. It's what I do. I'm a therapist, and a pretty good one at that, but I already resented him in a way for taking Kenny's last dime. I was looking forward to finding out what had happened to my lost lover—lost in every way it seemed. We hadn't seen each other in a few years, and didn't part on good terms. It all got too bizarre—too complicated—even for me.

I told him *he* needed therapy, but I wasn't going to be the one to help him sort out his life. That's when he said, in a tone of voice I'd never heard before, "There's nothing *to* sort out, so fuck off!"

I never saw Kenny again. I left in a huff never *wanting* to see him again. When things had simmered down though, I tried to get in touch with him over the next few months—texting, calling, emailing, and even writing a good old-fashioned letter. No response. I finally got up the nerve to go see him; I really *wanted* to see him, but I found he had moved and couldn't be found. The city is a big place, but isn't it incredible that a person can't be found—even if he doesn't want to be found. Kenny obviously did *not* want to be found.

So, Sam did show up; we shook hands, and I invited him into my inner sanctum—a quiet room with big cozy chairs, muted colors, diffused light from the windows in the day, and warm, soft lighting at night. I had created a place where my clients would feel comfortable and safe (I despise those words, "comfortable" and "safe"), so they would tell me their life stories, or at least the part of the story before the turning point, or after it—as the case might be.

"Hey, Sam, before you tell me about yourself, I'd like to ask something about Kenny. Do you mind?"

"No, Doc, no, I don't mind at all. Whadaya wanna know?"

"Well, you said Kenny gave you money before he was homeless, but how do you know he is homeless?"

"Well, I saw 'im a few days after that night I was at his place…the night he gave me the money. Boy, was I surprised when he did that, but I wasn't surprised ta see 'im on the streets."

"Oh, why was that?"

"Well, 'cause I didn't even know he *had* any money."

"No, I wanted to know why you weren't surprised to see Kenny homeless. I mean…you were friends, right?"

"No, we weren't what I'd call good friends or anythin' like that. He hung out with us at the shelter downtown, so we all knew 'im; he was always so nice ta us. But when I saw his place that night, it was a mess, and I kinda felt I was in better shape than him, and he didn't look too good either."

"So, you are homeless too, Sam?"

"Oh, no, no, but kinda down on my luck these days. I have a place, but went ta the shelter for meals sometimes…after I lost my job, ya know. That's where I met Kenny. He talked ta us…never seemed like he belonged there. I didn't mean ta, but I kinda whined about my sob story one night, and that's when he brought me back ta 'is place…probably on the worst night a my life, and gave me the money, and your number…said you'd help me. I went back ta thank 'im again a couple a days later. I knocked. No answer, so I was ready ta leave, when this guy across the hall comes out and tells me Kenny don't live there no more. I saw 'im on the street later, and that's when he told me he was homeless."

"Oh, I see…but…"

"I lied to ya, Doc," Sam interrupted. "'cause Kenny…he really gave me two thousand cash, but I used five hundred for my rent. When I saw 'im on the street, I told 'im, I says ta 'im, I says, you take the resta the money back, 'cause looks like ya need it more than me, but he wouldn't. That's when he told me he inherited some money and was givin it all away. He said he only wished he had more ta give…said he didn't need it. Jeez, can ya believe that?"

"Why didn't you just keep the money and not come here?" I asked, sort of wondering out loud.

With child-like innocence, Sam said, "Well, Kenny told me ta come see ya; that's why he gave me the money, ya know, in the first place. He said you'd help me."

"I will certainly do my best," and we began our first session.

It felt strange taking Kenny's money for my services. I offered to charge only half the amount for the sessions, so Sam could go beyond the fifteen weeks it would cover at my regular rate, but he wouldn't hear of it. As the weeks went by, I didn't learn much more about Kenny, but I learned a whole lot about Sam. He was a simple soul and honorable. I would keep him on when his money ran out. I hoped he would agree if he felt he needed more time. He was making progress though. He had found a job to keep him afloat, so he didn't have to go to the shelter for meals, but stops by once in a while to see the old gang. No sign of Kenny though; no one else had seen him either.

"He just disappeared," Sam said.

"And how do you feel about that?" I asked, but was thinking, *Yeah, I get it. That's what he did with me too—just disappeared.*

᠀

Kenny and I met when we were at Columbia, finishing up our degrees—his in philosophy and mine in clinical psychology. It was love at first sight you could say. I was amazed to realize there really *was* such a thing—that unexplainable kind of attraction. He was intriguing, quirky, quiet mostly—not the small-talk type, but I liked that. I thought later, *if I had wanted "normal," I would have looked for normal.* No such thing anyway, I know that for a fact.

His hair was dark and wild, and his eyes were kind —a soft, misty brown. His skin was clear and smooth, like a boy's, and his hands were perfection. I had the impression they were the kind a monk might have had— made for writing on parchment with a feather pen dipped into a pale blue glass inkwell. Later, I saw that his handwriting did have a grace and elegance about it, reminiscent of those Medieval illuminated manuscripts, and he did most of his writing by hand.

He wrote on various, obscure, abstract subjects— scholarly critiques on philosophy, theology and the lives of saints. He was intrigued with hagiography. He would tell me about the insights and revelations he had through his research and study. I loved the intensity of how he looked when he spoke of his work, and how he expressed ideas in such beautiful images, precise analogies, lofty metaphors and clear logic.

Who cared if our attraction was hormones or pheromones, and not destiny? I don't know how he would have described me, or what part of my body he may have thought was perfection, if any, but the feeling was mutual, passionate, intense—and ultimately doomed. There must have been a genetic code for disaster in the nature of our relationship. We were too different, and he gradually ascended or descended, depending on how you look at it, into an unreachable place, intent it seemed, on becoming a saint himself.

It wasn't going to work. His mind was like a black hole—sucking everything in. Nothing escaped—ideas, facts, implications, probabilities and possibilities. Mine was more like a sieve, holding only what I needed to get through each day,.the rest sifted through. Anyway, it's how I came to think of us as opposites.

Despite the chemistry, or maybe because of it, it had to come crashing down.

"You know what your trouble is, Kenny?" I said during one of our increasingly heated conversations. "Despite your knowledge of philosophy and religion and all, you don't really believe in anything, do you?"

We were sitting on his bed in the little room he was renting in the city, piled high with books, strewn with empty wine bottles, half-written papers and ashtrays crammed with cigarette butts on his desk. He got up, bare-legged in his white boxer shorts. I was already sorry I said anything and wished we were still in the bed together, so I could put my fingers through his matted hair and wrap my legs around his. He put his hands on his hips, made a half turn away then back again glaring at me with those eyes, always shining with an unearthly—maybe even heavenly gaze.

Almost in a whisper as if to himself, and with a look on his face like he was having another revelation, he said, "It's not that I don't believe in anything. I believe in *everything*!"

It was hard to have a saint for a lover, and it must have been even harder for him with me, a materialist and born therapist, analyzing him in a way no therapist would if she wanted to keep her client. But I *wasn't* his therapist; I was his lover and his anchor. I believed that. I had this weird thought. I was him trying to get in, and he was me trying to get out. I needed his ability to soar above it all—to what he might have called the "world of ideas," which transcended creation—the only reality to speak of, according to Saint Kenny.

If he needed me at all, maybe it was for my ability to focus on one thing at a time, to plan and to follow through. Kenny said we complimented each other. He said I thought inductively—from the specific to the general, and he thought deductively—from the general to the specific. Boy, was he deep, which I figured made me shallow—in my ambition to own my own practice; to make a good living; shallow in my wish to own a piece of real estate in some remarkable location, and in my need to take long weekends and vacations when I could get away. My desire for and my pleasure in material things, and all the rest of it, was in direct opposition to what Kenny stood for.

Like I said, we were doomed.

That started to become clear after a few days we spent at his Aunt Molly's. To me it was paradise: the island in the sea, the blue sky above, brilliant sun pouring through a dream house. I made a big fuss about it, and told Kenny I could see us living our lives there. I was like a mystic in ecstasy, but not the kind Kenny read about in his Medieval texts. I knew he could have been just as happy in one of those remote, monastic beehive huts on Skellig Michael off the coast of Ireland—happiest most likely.

I snuggled up to him on our first night there. The ocean breeze was cool, the full moon over the ocean—visible from our bed. The fragrance of beach roses and hedge, our bodies warm together, I put my head on his chest—which was also pretty perfect.

"What do you say, Ken? Let's live here. I'll set up a practice. You could work on your studies, maybe finish a book in the quiet of this place—that book you've been working on."

"It isn't a book; it's my theories and my musings."

"You've just been musing all this time, really? Didn't you ever think of sharing what you've learned, what you know?"

I'd been wondering for a while where he was going with his writing, along with a lot of other things I never dared mention.

"No, I *haven't* thought of it. I'm happy doing what I'm doing, and I don't want to leave the city. I like the noise and the grit of it and the people—the movement of their comings and goings, even the ones who have nowhere to go or nobody to be. I've been thinking about doing something else too, instead of living for myself. There is so much need out there."

"You mean like I do—live for myself?" I thought I knew where this was going, and me ruining the moment—again.

"No, I didn't mean that; you *do* help people, and that's a good thing. I want to do that too."

"I didn't know you thought of me as helping anyone. I mean, I certainly try." I was touched by his comment, suggesting out loud that my work was worthy after all.

"I don't think I'm the greatest example of good tough; that's for sure." I reminded him, "You've read, and know so well, the best of the best for inspiration on that score: Plato, Augustine, Aquinas, the saints…I mean."

"Well, I've read about their ideas and experiences, yes, but I need to do something with them."

I silently agreed.When we got back to the city, at first he continued to live in his dark room, thinking and writing. He still was doing some part time work in a library, barely earning enough to subsist—subsidized by me, which I didn't mind. I still admired his ideals, and I loved him—meaning I made sure we could both live the life I wanted—dinners, plays, trips, none of which seemed to matter much to Kenny.

Soon after, he began walking the streets at night encountering those who could use something good in their lives. When he started bringing back lost souls, disheveled and sometimes incoherent ones with wild eyes, I began to question his judgement, and wondered if there was room for me in his future. I know how that sounds, but I was shaken by it all, and not only for my own well being. I also questioned Kenny on a finer point.

"You may be giving these souls something to eat or a coat to wear, but are you effecting any real change in their lives?" I had to ask.

"It doesn't *matter* if their lives change," he almost shouted. "That's your goal, not mine. I'm happy to help in small ways...in immediate need. You manipulate people and want them to live as you do."

"Now, wait a minute," I shouted back, feeling blindsided. "You said before that I did good, and I thought you meant it. Why are you being so hostile now?" There were other words spoken or shouted back and forth, and that's when I practically screamed that he needed a therapist.

It was the last thing I ever said to him.

We parted ways, and that, as they say, was that. I thought I had come to accept it was all for the best. Kenny was right; I *had* wanted him to live as I did. I didn't want to, and could not live as he did.

On the fifteenth week of Sam's therapy, he reminded me that it was our intended last session,.."Well, this is it, Doc, the grand finoulie." It sort of took me by surprise, though I had to agree he was in a good place.

"Well, you let me know, Sam, if you need to come in again, and remember what I said—no charge, okay?"

"Yeah, yeah, sure thing, and thanks, Doc," he said in his usual, matter-of-fact way.

I had looked forward to our sessions. I liked Sam. He has a natural kind of wisdom, and it didn't take much to get him to think about things in another way, so he was able to make some positive changes. He had been in a rut, but was easily budged out of it. I would miss him; having him around made me feel close to Kenny—strange as that sounds.

"Okay, Sam, you take care, now. He hesitated, then pulled an envelope out of his pocket and handed it to me.

"What's this?"

"I dunno, but Kenny said ta give it ta ya after we had our last meetin, so here it is, Doc."

Looking back, I don't remember Sam's leaving the office. I just stood staring down at the envelope in my trembling hand. I don't know how long it was before I fell into one of those cozy chairs to open it. So much time had passed since we were together, but no love lost on my side. *Was it a suicide note?* I found myself thinking crazy things the moment before I opened it, desperately hoping it was the impossible—an invitation to meet him somewhere, anywhere. I wanted to look into those eyes once more. Those old feelings, memories and desire had been rushing in over the past weeks—flooding in and swirling around in my head and in my heart.

❦

That was two years ago. I am still grieving. The letter Sam gave me was from a law firm, and was a shocker. Kenny had willed Aunt Molly's house to me! When I went to see the attorney, she told me she had met with Kenny only once, and didn't know that much about him, except that he had been ill, even before the inheritance from his aunt. That explains his giving a fortune away, but why will the house to me—after all this time?

I'm settled into my new practice on Martha's Vineyard. I may never know, but I have been hoping to find clues among the things Kenny left in this room overlooking the sea, the one we stayed in that night. The desk is piled with his writings, overflowing shelves of books, stacked boxes of papers, all for me to live with— alone.

Today, I found that letter I had written to Kenny years ago. When I unfolded it, a piece of parchment fell out. On it, in his beautiful script, were these lines:

> *I cannot live with you—*
> *It would be life—*
> *And life is over there—*
> *Behind the shelf—*
>
> *So We must meet apart—*
> *You there—I—here—*
> *With just the Door ajar*
> *Oceans are—and Prayer—*
> *And that White Sustenance—*
> *Despair—*

Isn't that the truth? Not exactly a clue, though— more of a confirmation of what I already knew.

Now I can't get those lines out of my head.

God is Love
Of a man returning to his childhood home for atonement

Driving for hours, he starts to wonder if the road stretching ahead is endless. His anxiety building—like when he first tried to grasp the idea of "forever," or envision the universe expanding outward—into what, into where? Colors and shapes blur together and fade: tree branches into sky; gravel edging the road into fields of dried cornstalks. Wispy clouds line the glowing horizon at sunset as he travels west. This is how he remembers it in the cold season.

He is going back after so many years. He doesn't know what he will see, or what he will say, but he needs to close the circle of his life, "whose center is everywhere and circumference nowhere."

By early morning, he sees the farmhouse rising darkly against a brightening sky. His eyes fix it as he turns on to the long, narrow earthen drive. The fence on the perimeter is broken in some places, missing in others; some of the once-sheltering oaks are gone. They have been living only in his memory, but the old poplars still stand on either side of the front porch, with its wooden steps sagging into the damp earth. Twisting bramble and weeds crowd the flower gardens that once grew in sunny spots.

Ahead, loom rusted parts of yellow and green farm equipment, abandoned near the barn with part of the roof down on one side. He sees the fading painted image covering the top half of the barn facing the house, the first thing he saw each morning from his bedroom window: a red cross against shafts of light, over which the words are printed:

GOD IS LOVE.

He remains in the car, his eyes closed, until he shivers from the cold. Emerging, he walks toward the house, observing broken windows, warped siding, and fallen shingles on the path to the back door. Entering the low doorway, he bends in a gesture of forced humility.

There is the wide stone hearth, charred ends of logs still across a blackened grate. Here is where the oak table stood, he and his sister set for Sunday dinners. He stops, moves his hand over the place where it had been. Entering the front room, he scans the whole of it camera-wise. Tall windows line the west wall where, on summer afternoons, he would read stretched out on the window seat below, imagining he was drifting to a sun-soaked Greek isle.

The windows, coated with a fine yellow film, diffuse the light through the vacant room. He sees, not the empty space, but everything as it had been on the day he left—with no warning, no word. A rocking chair next to the fireplace; an old-style standing radio the family would gather round to listening to hymns on Sunday evenings;

a sofa opposite the fireplace; his father's straight-backed chair with its black, crackled leather seat; a marble-topped table with frosted globe lamp painted with peonies, matching the ones on the wall paper—now worn in places down to the plaster. How elated and proud his mother had been when she papered the walls herself, saying, "There, now we have a proper sitting room."

All the while, his memory projects a tableau of intimate vignettes and voices from the past into the room that smells of earth and cold, and feels like pain. He has arrived—returned from another world to speak to his God-fearing family, who had raised him to work on the land, making sure he was educated enough to run the farm. All gone now, they had waited years for his return. He has to believe they will gather here again, in spirit to listen to what he has come to say.

Outside, the wind kicks up, whining through the house, rattling the remaining shutters. His fingers, though gloved, are numb. He heads outside to gather kindling. Tiny vortices of golden dust rise up here and there as he picks up broken branches and twigs to build a fire to warm the frigid room. When the fire blazes, in the glowing warmth of its flames, he conjures his imaginary family, summoning them to hear the truth of his life.

He wonders, *Is reconciliation more possible with spirits than with living beings?*

There is his mother, seated at the front windows, gazing out; his father stands at her side. His sister, Anna curls on the rocker next to the fire, his abandoned lover on the threshold, her back to the room. He can't recall her face —only her despair.

He wants to say, "Call me Ishmael, Gilgamesh, Oedipus. I have seen the white whale, entered the cedar forest, solved the famous riddle." But, those are his inspirations; they never would understand. He will speak in plain language, though those epic figures and their stories still live within him, the foundation for his thinking about the world, life, and himself.

To the conjured visions now assembled for his homecoming, he states his case:

"When I was a boy, I read about heroes' journeys, and I knew I had to set out on my own. I don't think of myself as a hero, but I do think that simply living life is heroic, contending with all the forces coming against it. Here I am…battle-weary from forging my own path. I have survived, as I must believe you also have. There is no end to our journeys, here or beyond. There is always still a far way to go."

He had set out long ago, leaving everything behind, toward what he had hoped would foster consciousness and conscience. He freed himself to leave the known for what was out there yet to be discovered, and to acquire an understanding of what it is to be human, which his youthful readings and musings had begun to suggest.

"I strove toward a vision, but...I am flawed, still so flawed." His tale unravels, partly in sorrow without remorse, partly in victory without joy. "Maybe it is I who need to hear my own story to grasp it, but I put it before you," he, hoping in whatever feeble way, he might atone for the pain he had caused.

"I wasn't ungrateful or, at least, I never connected what I did or didn't do with ingratitude." Early on, he knew he would not replay the worn record of his father's life and his father's before him.

He intends to acknowledge to his sister the he abandoned her, after the confidences they had shared. He wants to kneel before his mother to ask forgiveness for his "mysterious disappearance," for her never to have looked upon his face again, for his not having fulfilled her reasonable expectation that her family remain near, and that life go on in the same way ever after.

He thought to apologize to his young lover, whose beauty and innocence must have long ago faded. Her words, screamed to him still resounding, "If you leave me, I'll hang myself from the barn rafters."

"No, no you won't! Don't say that," he had shouted back, feeling held hostage to others' expectations and needs, but also bound to them by love. "I can't stay to save everyone else and lose my self." The next day, with guilt and grief, but with the vision of the life before him, he did the thing he had to do.

"I veered off the trajectory created for me…set sail on my own voyage, uncharted and blown off course many times," as he remembered his wish to see wide rivers, not content with irrigation ditches and small streams trickling through the countryside: "I wanted to see the Nile, the Amazon, cities rising against the sky: Athens, Paris. I wanted to meet people who didn't live as we did in what I had come to think of as this God-forsaken place."

His mother had said it was *not* God-forsaken, "God is everywhere the eye can see and the heart can feel—horizon to horizon." If that is so, he tried to reason with her, couldn't He then be found in other lands and landscapes—ones that would better serve to shape and grow something still small inside himself? He wanted to see the open ocean, stand before and climb mountains, meet and get to know people not like him, people who might be God and angels in disguise—strangers who would become his guests.

"When I finally settled after years of wandering, it was on that island on the wide Hudson. I felt I had found my place…my home." There he saw those driven in black limos stopping at hotels, theaters and restaurants. "I made my way among them, but mingled with those who had lost their way, but not their souls." To those he had dedicated himself—those who carried the sum of their lives in carts or plastic bags, maybe disguising sainthood beneath blank and somber eyes.

"How can I tell you what it would have meant for me to have stayed here? What it has meant for me to have done what I did, see what I have seen? I did what I had to do...trade the predictable for...for the possible. Here, yes, I was secure and comfortable, but... I didn't want that. I...I didn't know what I would wanted, or what I would find, only that I needed the unpredictable...and some sense of fulfillment."

He turns toward the windows, "Mother, you said I was a dreamer, a doubter, selfish. Father, you said I was lazy, a sinner, a bad influence on Anna with my wild talk of journeys and trials...that I was wasting my time reading what you called 'those foolish books.'"

Then to Anna, "I have prayed you found your way and lived a life *you* chose," as they had often encouraged each other to do, but wondering through the years if she had instead submitted to the life laid out before them. Had she been left utterly alone?

He glanced at the figure in the shadowy doorway, but could say nothing, the snare of her last words to him having left a crusted over wound on his heart.

He paused until he could recall the urgency that had propelled him beyond all considerations to leave, and how the ideas in those books became ideals to be acted upon—light-filled thoughts that opened up all the color of dreams, inspiring his plan to free himself, body, and soul.

"When I was a boy, I loved this house…the picnics, the Sunday prayers, the hymns, and I always loved you… all. I knew what you wanted for me, and…I *wanted* to be good, to be grateful." How he had struggled to be obedient, to honor father and mother—the commandment they repeated almost daily, noting the fires of hell awaited those who transgressed it, or any of the other nine "shall" and "shall nots," until he could obey only one commandment: to experience life by following the fire within him.

"Please, Mother, I know you thought I should be content to be here, where I was born, but I…I had to walk into the world…on the narrow path of my own making… my own…limitations. I guess I…I had to learn things the hard way, and not just believe or follow all the things you tried to teach me. I couldn't live up to what everyone else expected. I had my own expectations, and have come to believe as certainly as you had in your beliefs."

He speaks what he could not articulate before he had lived it. "We have not come to earth to blindly fulfill the dictates of God or man, ignoring our own experience, avoiding our own thoughts and questions, denying our doubts. Wouldn't an omniscient God have foreseen, even intended rebellion? The disobedience of Adam and Eve was not sin, but a picture of destiny, human destiny—to be cast out of a perfect garden, to lose our innocence and to learn through suffering. To be fully human is to choose the good—in freedom, not out of command or fear.

If I hadn't left, how else would I have come to know that evil is a mystery woven into the very fabric of the universe? Evil is not so much to be resisted but endured. Good and evil are all mixed up, one can be mistaken for the other, and what we think is good may turn to bad, while our good intentions can affect others in ways we couldn't have imagined, no matter what we intended."

He knows his own rebellion, by default or design, has moved toward his becoming "one with the Father" and was meant to achieve that fulfillment alone.

"I wanted to find my own fulfillment. And I did once…for a while. At least the kind I had imagined could be mine, with a red-haired woman I loved too much. She painted my portrait in blue with a gold halo. That was before our son was born with his spine outside of his body," he swallowed hard. "On the first anniversary of his death, I came home to find…she was gone." For the first time, the realization comes to him with excruciating clarity that *she* had vanished, just as he had from the sad farmhouse in which he now stands. He had never spoken the words out loud before—until now.

"I burned the portrait, along with the letters I had written each day for a year, with nowhere to send them. What would I do with all the love remaining?

"I had wanted to find life—as if it were something to find rather than to live…too proud in my belief…or my illusion that I was destined somehow to find fulfillment. Instead I lived alone with yet another mystery, until I took in a young man in rags with violet eyes who danced in night in St. Mark's Place—asking nothing in return for his performances of grace and beauty—but a witness."He had meant to speak many more things into the quiet room to those he imagines are listening now. He is spent, empty to speak of the years roaming the city streets, to which he will return after this pilgrimage to the past—maybe stronger, maybe more broken.

All at once his life appears before him—as a sacrifice, forfeiting simplicity for the sublime, facts for hard-won knowledge. With the vision, comes a warmth, a calm, the frosted breath of his words visible, his voice hollow and weak.

"I am sorry for the pain I caused and…wish only… that peace be with you—now and forever." And he feels it is so.

The wind has died down, the fire gone to embers. Across the fields, the sun is low in the late afternoon sky. The circle is closed, he on the outside, the imaginary figures fading into the darkening room.

On This Ground
Of a mother grieving for her lost son

Nora was comforted to know Indians had once danced on the ground where her son had taken his last breath. She did not discover that until today, after wondering all through summer and fall if she had somehow imagined his death. Since that rainy evening she had slept on the sofa in the front room with the shades up, waiting to see him coming up the walkway or to hear him open the door.

When she arrived at the accident scene that night, she saw the chalked outline of his body. Only an hour before, at the hospital, his young face was at peace. She was given a blue plastic bag containing his sweatshirt, keys, cigarette lighter, wallet, phone, some change, and an arrowhead he always carried with him.

She reached for the sweatshirt, held it to her face, inhaled, and pulled it over her head. She walked the few steps to the chalked outline and lay down within it on the wet, leaf-strewn sidewalk.

In his last moments, did he suffer, think of me, call out, pray? Did he know he would die, hope he would live? Was he already unconscious when he was thrown from the car?

These were questions Nora lived with and sometimes spoke out loud or wrote down over and over again on sleepless nights. She thought of all the times she had held him, comforted him when he was a boy. In the end he was alone.

This morning in late December, she awakens to the crisp stillness before a snow. This is the day of winter solstice with lengthening days ahead. With that promise of light, it comes to her so clearly, she must to go to where the chalk outline has long faded, where no trace of shattered glass remains.

Only burning grief remains. Each day upon wakening it assails her, but on this morning she feels moved to give over to time and reason. *He is not going to call; He is not going to walk past the window. He is not coming home.*

Feeling an urgency, she dresses, pulls the shades down on the front windows and locks the door. It irritates her when the phone rings.

"Hi, Addie, what's up?"

"Hey, Mom. Nothing much. How are you?"

"Good. I'm good; how about you?"

"I'm fine just checking in. They're calling for snow today."

"Oh?" Nora looks out the window. "I see it's flurrying already. You'll be happy to know I'm going for a walk."

It's a revelation to Addie. Partly elated that her mother plans to do anything at all, other than wait, and partly concerned at the sudden change. "What, where? I mean that's great, Mom, but the snow. How about if I come over and we walk together like we used to, or maybe we could just have coffee and walk tomorrow?"

"No, no, I'll be fine. I have to go today. I'm leaving now for Three Island Cove," already sorry she has told Addie where she is headed. "See you tonight though, right?"

"No, I mean yes, you will see me tonight, but... Mom, wait. I'll be right over. Don't go without me. You shouldn't go by yourself."

"Now, don't worry. You've been telling me to get out and do something, and now I am. See you tonight."

"I...I wanna go with..."

Nora hangs up, hoping Addie won't show up at the cove. She knows it's been hard for Addie too, and that maybe she has made it harder on her, but grief is a *private* matter, to be protected not shared—not even with her own daughter—her "favorite," as Andrew used to say.

She enters Andrew's darkened room, which remains as it was on the night he left and never returned: curtains drawn; an unmade bed; video games; on the floor; empty cigarette pack, and batteries on the bedside table. A job application and resume on his desk remind her that, in his slow, deliberate way, Andrew was ready to make changes in his life.

Each morning since his death, she calls into the room, "good morning," and in the evening a "good night," but not today. She goes for the blue bag at the foot of the bed, takes out the sweatshirt, holds it close to her once again, lifts it to her lips, then slips it on. She hurries to the hall closet for coat, hat and gloves and steps out into the cold air, emerging into what seems like a new world.

It's just the old world I hardly recognize, where people have been going places and doing things, living their lives as usual. For her, there has been no usual, no place to go, nothing to do and no life to live—only her world of grief—vast and deep.

It's so quiet, so white, so pure.

Her senses open on the deserted street, where holiday lights glimmer from houses and trees. Head down against the wind, she sees snowflakes sparkle, then fade on the sidewalk. She hears the sounds of icy branches stirring in the wind and her quickening breath, as it turns to frosty mist in front of her. The pace of her lengthening stride uphill sets her heart pounding; a burning cold fills her lungs.

Disoriented by the opening of the forgotten world outside herself, she also begins to sense something inside —unwanted and unwelcome. Out of her inner landscape, there seem to be thought threads being cast backward in time, attaching to images, people, places and events—connecting her with her son. Her impulse is to turn around and head back to the familiar stasis of home, but her intuition and the intensity of the experience compels her: *Keep going.*

What is this feeling of contracting and expanding at the same time? These intimations of truths, both light and dark? Were those days and nights of ritual sorrow preparing the ground for all that flows from her now? Maybe, yes. Something is shifting. Why? To where? Threads of questions, regrets, love and loss stream out, weave together; emotion gushes in waves, leaving her breathless— a deluge to drown in.

The widening circumference of memory touches many truths, exposes illusions, illuminates things forgotten, brings the yet unknown to the surface. Nora had not wanted a second child.

Was that really twenty years ago? I don't know why, but when Addie was born, I felt normal, whole again. She brought me down to earth. A beautiful gift, taking away the darkness. Life was bearable again, redemption for past transgressions. With Andrew, I had to reach into myself…find strengths I didn't know I have. Matt said I saw everything too dark or too light… deluded myself. I knew he was right, but couldn't let him know that he knew me that well.

She remembers that, as a baby Andrew had been content but less responsive to affection than was Addie. He didn't like to be held and was often ill. A dreamy, independent, willful and irritable child, he tried her patience. More than that, as he grew, she felt he was asking her to change in order to see who *he* was, to discover what he needed, which was hard—maybe impossible.

Matt said Andrew was my "project." He wanted no part in it, wasn't interested in my one-woman show. I shut him out — and everybody and everything else too.

Early on there had been signs that, while Andrew may not have been as "awake" as Addie, he had extraordinary insight about the essence and purpose of things. Nora felt he was a puzzle, a paradox and, in many ways, knew more about life than she did. His intuition and sensitive nature engendered a deep love in her, but an uneasy one. Something was asked in exchange. She tried to figure out what it was, but never had. She became convinced Andrew's inherent wisdom was meant to guide his parents to discover parts of themselves that were missing, to the self-knowledge they lacked. His father did not agree, insisting that nothing had to be done—except to live their lives.

I didn't have to push Matt away like that....I shouldn't have. I miss him terribly. There, I've said it. He was right. I created my own Greek tragedy, got in my own way, and in Andrew's too. It wasn't a good place to be, above all things like that. I felt Addie had lifted a burden, but I guess I just placed it on Andrew instead. He had to tolerate my mothering and smothering; suffer for Matt's leaving us; for my trying to be father and mother; for our move away from the only home he had ever known and loved. Did he carry that resentment to his death? And I never got the chance to....I failed him in every way.

"Oh, Andrew, can you forgive me?" she asks out loud.

By the time she reaches the place she had dreaded, but at which she longed to be, a perfect, almost visible imagination had formed. Perfect in that it is whole, woven in reverse from moments in time, expanding outward, encompassing the lives of a mother, a son, and a family—then, now and forever.

Looking up, she notices a sign post rising from the pavement—one of those placards noting some bit of history.

Why haven't I seen this before? Was it always here?

SAMUEL DE CHAMPLAIN. Due east from here on July 16, 1605, the Sieur de Monts sent Samuel de Champlain ashore to parley with some Indians. They danced for him and traced an outline map of Massachusetts Bay.

Nora remains for some time gazing at the sign with the new-found realization that long ago something extraordinary took place here. An exchange, a sharing, a trust, an encounter between the strangers who had arrived on a foreign shore and the Native Americans who danced to welcome them, and shared their knowledge of the land —a living knowledge inside of them.

She reaches down to touch the ground.

And it was here, too, where another soul had departed—Andrew, whom she had both striven to know and to become more like.

Has he united with the others from another time?

In an instant, she *became* the bare trees, the grey sky and the falling snow, a small but integral part within creation, which holds all that was, is and will be.

"Time," Nora smiles, "another illusion. We are all here—then and now and tomorrow."

How long she remained in this reverie of her own creation, in the light of the knowledge the placard had shed, who can say?

A few snowflakes float down like feathers. Feeling the cold more than before, even though the wind has subsided, she turns, glances back, then begins walking quickly downhill.

There is Addie coming toward her, smiling and waving as she makes her way amid the lights twinkling from trees and houses along the still, quiet street.

Broken Beads ~ Blue Sky
Of a teacher finding strength in broken things

Her mother's beads broke and scattered across the floor backstage. Four strands of rose-colored iridescent beads, a tiny crystal between each and with a gold filigree clasp. She remembers gazing at them, touching them, rolling them in her small fingers as she sat on her mother's lap. That was so many years ago.

When Christina was twenty-one, her mother had warned, "Don't marry that man," but she did.

On her wedding day, only a few months after her mother had died from an aggressive cancer, she had begged her father, "Don't let that woman sit next to you where Mom was supposed to be," but he did.

On her honeymoon, under a clear blue sky on an island beach, she lay on her tie-dyed scarf, the sun beating down, a cool breeze off the surf, high tide rolling in. She had called to her husband who walked along the waves, "Don't be long," but he was. She waited—alone until the sun was going down, wind chilling her to the bone. The once cloudless sky now resembled the transparent scarf wrapped around her shoulders: fading blue, streaked with grey and yellow, which made her cry.

Since then, he has been "disappearing," leaving her to wonder and worry.

Where does he go? How long will it be until he returns? Does he ever realize he is missed, or even that he is expected back at all? Doesn't he remember he was going to finish fixing that door, that he was supposed to meet me for lunch, that he will miss dinner with the family—again?

Whenever she tried to sort out the how and why of it, her thoughts raced to a vanishing point. She told herself it didn't matter after all.

What worried her most was her husband's patients arriving when he might not be there to receive them. One day, she cancelled the few remaining appointments. After several doctors' visits, she and her husband learned there was good reason for his behavior which prompted his early retirement. Still, discovery of the reason for the years of disappearances and seemingly random, inconsiderate antics didn't change things much. Even with medication and therapy, there would be no quick fix, no perfect ending. It was she who had to adjust. It was she who struggled to transform denial into acceptance, impatience into tolerance, and resentment into understanding—hateful contraries.

These are the thoughts arising in Christina as she collects the scattered beads. She had brought them in with the other pieces of her mother's jewelry for the high school girls to wear in their roles as aristocratic Victorian ladies. After the play, one careless girl in a hurry tugged at those strands of memories, sending them into the shadows behind the curtains.

I'll take them for repair to be strung back together, all four strands—like new. What is wrong with that girl anyway?

Christina liked finding purpose for the things she had salvaged from her childhood home in a forlorn, upstate New York town. Besides the jewelry, she has a yellow Bakelite clock in the shape of a teapot in her kitchen above the stove. Six ruby red wine glasses, a set of dishes trimmed with dogwood flowers, and hand-painted Italian bowls, all arranged in a glass-front cabinet, as her mother had kept them. Most cherished are old letters and cards found in her mother's desk after the funeral— touchable memories to take into her hands and hold to her heart, a comfort when she can't mange to be accepting, tolerant or understanding.

Driving home this night, she comes back again and again to brokenness: *Things are coming apart.* That very morning, as she dressed for the long day ahead, she brushed against and dislodged the small plate hanging on the wall—the one her mother had given her before entering the hospital for the last time. On the sky-blue and white memento, in silvery script was: Baby Christina Marie ~ Born November 10, 1974 ~ 7 pounds 3 ounces. She left it shattered on the floor.

Almost home now, she loosens her fingers on the wheel as she drives down the tree-lined street. She recalls the sense of freedom she once had felt driving east on the Massachusetts turnpike to her uncharted life—to all that lay ahead of her, singing out, "Boston, you're my home." Later, she found she had to get away from her new home when, once too often, her husband did not show up for dinner; or she again had to make excuses to angry patients; or he had forgotten to call for heating oil, and she came home to a frigid house. Then there were those maddening, one-sided conversations, constant distractions and interruptions, unrelated questions and non-sequiturs until she had to laugh—or go insane.

Who am I living with anyway, Salvador Dali?

She usually laughed, but when she could not, it was time to flee. She would pack up the car and head west with her two small children to visit her father, which also meant seeing the woman he married—now her step mother, who without a shred of consideration for the motherless bride's request, saw fit to take her "rightful place" next to Christina's father in the church pew.

During one of those spontaneous trips, that woman called Christina selfish and disrespectful when Christina had said, "I'd like the kids to eat before Dad gets home. They are usually in bed by eight, and it's been a long day, with the drive and all."

"Well, your father won't be here till eight-thirty, so they'll *have* to wait. It won't kill them to not get their way —for once."

Christina bit her bottom lip, ignored the comment and continued setting the table, as her mother had always done. She spread a crisp white cloth. She found the familiar white dishes with an ivy border pushed to the back of the kitchen cabinet. She took pleasure in placing them around the table, as if she were still a girl at home on a school evening.

"I don't think Dad would mind if the children ate early, Charlotte," she tried to reason, and called the children to come to the table. Before the words were out, she felt the sharp sting of Charlotte's hand across her cheek.

"You never did have an ounce of respect. Well, you are not the crowned princess around *here* anymore."

Christina dropped the plate she was holding, put her hand up to her face and blinked back the hot tears welling up, so the children wouldn't see. But they had heard Charlotte's harsh words. They saw the broken plate and their mother leaning over to pick up the pieces.

Charlotte grabbed the plates already on the table and the shards from Christina's trembling hands and tossed them into the trash. "There, I've been meaning to throw those old things away," she said, as she removed drab brown dishes from the cabinet, held them out to Christina, and pointed to mismatched glasses on the shelf, two with Peter Pan and the Darling children flying away, and three others with watermelon slices.

"Now, finish the job, and we'll wait for your father to come home."

Christina mechanically went around the table with the dishes and glasses, taking solace in thinking of her mother's thin-stemmed, ruby red glasses in her own cabinet at home.

Can people just be replaced like broken china?

In the quiet of night, she returned to the kitchen, took the plates out of the trash, and put them into her suitcase, intending to mend the broken ones when she got home.

She loved her father deeply, despite his betrayal and "o'er hasty marriage" where, "the funeral baked meats did coldly furnish forth the marriage tables," lines from *Hamlet* she had quoted to her husband on the day of what they have since referred to as, "the unholy union."

Scenes of that incident, her wedding day and sitting on the beach at sunset linger now. She shudders at the memory of them. Then she remembers how, when her father arrived home that evening, he smiled, hugged her and said he was glad she had "come home," though it never felt like home again without her mother.

Home. Is it a place or a feeling?

She is glad the day is at an end, and that there is a parking place to be had. Gathering up the bags in the back seat, she hears the rustle of leaves from the chestnut tree at the curb's edge—a welcome in the balmy night air. She stops with a sigh to look up at the few steps to the porch, feeling worn out and on edge. At least a small weight had lifted with her director duties completed for the school year.

She manages the steps, opens the front door and climbs the staircase to the second floor. Facing her at the landing are two doors. The open one is to the shadowy office where streetlights cast dark reflections. Black branches dance on the ceiling and walls, like a crazy light show in the abandoned room. She pushes open the other door to the living room and drops the plastic bags containing a red paisley smoking jacket, a blue chiffon dress, black suede heels, a silver cigarette case, a blonde wig, a straw handbag, a bunch of yellow paper roses, a wooden jewelry box and a pink satin bag with the broken beads.

She intended to go straight to bed, but the sofa looks inviting. Too tired to walk the few extra feet to the bedroom, she flops down, picks up the remote and clicks to the classic movie channel. Staring at the TV screen, her mind drifts to a recent visit with a friend. As they walked along a windy beach, the tide rolling in over the deserted, narrow shore, Christina told her friend about the dreaded oncologist's appointment that day, and the diagnosis.

There was a long silence.

"They say, if we could see things from the highest perspective, it would all be good," her friend said.

It was thoughtless and rude of her to say that. Hadn't she just heard the bad news?

The friends had long confided in each other, exchanged ideas and experiences, pondering whether life has any meaning at all, and, if so, what it could be. They would look at each other and say, "It is what it is; it will be what it will be."

Now, it was different; Christina knew what was to be, and so did her friend.

To the background bantering of Hepburn and Tracey, she is remembering how she and her friend had read about and discussed reincarnation and karma, and considered it a more rational alternative to heaven or hell —or nothingness. They neither entirely believed, nor disbelieved, but were attracted to the idea that souls choose the circumstances of their existence before birth— ones that provide the context to live out their karma. They agreed everyone's life seems to have a theme and pattern, with recurring questions and challenges to guide them, maybe even to a certain destiny, but also there are choices to be made in life, informed by increasing consciousness and self-knowledge.

Still, for her friend to have suggested that *anything* could be good about her diagnosis was wrong. Thoughts crowd in, as she scans the cluttered room.

Is this my destiny? Did I choose it? Can I change it, fix it, get well? Is the highest perspective heaven? And why do I have to sink so low to get there? Do I know or believe anything?

Her husband shuffles in and stands in front of her. She is surprised to see he is still awake. Usually, he is on the sofa asleep or already in bed. After twenty years of marriage, there is still no predicting what she can count on him for, yet he loves her; she loves him. That much is never in question.

He is not unfaithful. He is not unkind, and he always wanders back home to her. It has just taken those years of adjusting and lowering expectations to realize that she can depend on him *only* for the things he is *able* to do, and not always for those she wishes for or needs.

Is that my karma, or his?

Her mind fogs over with the mystery of it all, grateful for those things he can manage.

"How'd it go?"

"Oh, the kids did a great job. We packed the house, and everyone loved it, but…I'm glad it's over." The broken beads still have her upset, but she doesn't have the energy to tell him about it.

"Want something to drink? There's some leftover pizza."

"No, I'm fine. Hey, are you coming with me tomorrow?"

" Ehh…what time?"

"My appointment is at two. I'll be home around one."

"I'll go with you," he says, padding back to the kitchen, then comes back with a glass of cranberry juice and a cold piece of pizza.

"I…I don't think I can eat…"

"I'm going to bed," he interrupts leaving the room.

"Okay, I'll be there in a few minutes," she calls back, wondering whether he will be around the next day when it is time to go to her first chemo treatment or if he will be AWOL again.

She leans back against the soft cushions, trying to focus on the last scenes of the film, unable to keep her eyes open for more than a few seconds at a time. When she opens them again, she sees, "THE END" in white letters on a grainy black background. She manages to rouse herself, but begins to dread another sleepless night. She sits staring at the bags on the floor, thinking again about high perspectives, low places, broken beads and dishes, karma and cancer treatments.

She wonders if she has the strength to undress, as she picks up the crumpled nightgown at the foot of the bed next to the shattered blue and white pieces on the floor. She turns away, eases into bed and edges back, against her husband until her legs touch his.

Tomorrow is another day, but not an ordinary one.

Images of her children's faces appear. It was the hardest thing telling her family—their sadness and apprehension of grief—another long silence. Her daughter was in tears, and her son said, "I want you to get well."

Her husband got up and walked away with his head down. The oncologist told her she would *not* get well, and would be in some kind of treatment for the remainder of time she had left. Since then, family talk has been only of practical matters: treatments, appointments, and the details of "getting things in order." She has shielded her son and daughter from most of it, taking on the burden of their pain, as well as her own.

Still, she has hope; she has the will to live, if not the strength to think about whatever she will have to endure with the treatments. She isn't sure how miracles fit into *her* life's theme, free will or destiny, but she believes in prayer and in miracles.

"Of everyone I've ever known," her friend had also said that day, "you are the bravest, strongest, most positive person."

Funny, I don't feel strong, positive or even like a person. She thought of herself, rather, as a shadow of the self she tried to build and sustain in this lifetime, with parts of herself missing, wavering, like the quivering branches on the ceiling of the abandoned room at the top of the stairs— a shadow of something real, but not real, caught between hope and despair—another uncharted place.

"You love life and live life," her friend had said that day, as if Christina needed a reminder, especially now. She also was left to ponder the other thing her friend had said, "It's not over till it's over."

She closes her eyes, whispers a prayer, listens to her husband's quiet breathing, as thoughts, feelings and images swirl together, fading into the dark future, into sleep.

In the hospital waiting room, she gazes out the window at the vast, clear blue and cloudless sky, holding the pink satin bag full of beads.

"Christina," a nurse calls and comes over to stand in front of her—blocking out the blue. "We're ready for you; come on back."

She looks at her husband—lost child—not even pretending to be strong for her. She wonders if he will come back when he is called to sit with her for the treatment, or if he will have wandered off. He lifts his hand and manages a smile, which she carries with her down the long hall and into the sterile room.

The nurse gets her settled on a bed turned up to a sitting position and prepares a bright red IV drip. Christina is grateful to be opposite a window with a view of blue sky.

In the closed palm of her hand, she holds a single rose-colored bead. She loves the feel of its round smoothness. It has nothing to do with the rest of the beads now. It is beautiful and perfect all on its own.

She closes her eyes, imagines herself bathed in the glow of its color, looking down from a very high place—a place where she sees everything exactly as it is.

Epilogue

LIPARI

When Helen completed her first collection of tales, *Book of Hours*—each one a prayer—she felt she had given the beings voice, set them free. There are many more waiting to be heard; of that she is certain.

It is not lost on her that the beings and their tales had found her, not in her beloved island home, but across the wide ocean, in a house that was not her home, in a town devoid of the kind of beauty that has become part of her, in a place she never loved as she loves Lipari.

Yet, it was there that they were waiting to find her. Or had she found them?

No matter.

She holds her book lovingly in her hands and opens it. She turns each page, then writes a note of greeting and gratitude to Earl Marchenmeister, Jr., and sends it off to Time & Tide Antique Clocks.

She is not surprised when it comes back, stamped: "Address Unknown."

Acknowledgements & Notes

BOOK OF HOURS
Page 15: "What man of you, having a hundred sheep…" from Luke 15:4-6, KJV

THE HOLES THEY LEAVE
Page 24: *"as above, so below"* from the Hermetic texts of the *Emerald Tablet* of Hermes Trismegistus.

Pages 25: "Each night I count the stars/…" by Amiri Baraka from "Preface to a Twenty Volume Suicide" in *S O S: POEMS 1961-2013*, copyright ©2014 The Estate of Amiri Baraka, with permission of Grove/Atlantic, Inc. Any third party use of this material outside of this publication is prohibited.

Page 26: "mystical moist night air" from "When I Heard the Learned Astronomer" by Walt Whitman.

Page 32: "That's how you came here/like a star…" from "A Star Without a Name" by Jalāl ad-Dīn Muhammad Rūmī (Mathnawi III, 1284 - 1288). Translation by Coleman Barks in *Say I Am You,* (copyright ©Maypop, 1994), with the express permission of Coleman Barks. Any third party use of this material outside of this publication is prohibited.

Page 36: "a thing with feathers…" from "Hope" by Emily Dickinson in *Poems by Emily Dickinson, First & Second Series*, Mabel Loomis Todd and T. W. Higginson, editors
.

_____"faithful, even as it fades from fullness/…" from "Faith" by David Whyte in *River Flow: New & Selected Poems*, with permission from Many Rivers Press. Any third party use of this material outside of this publication is prohibited.

Page 37: "constant sorrow" from"Man of Constant Sorrow" by Dick Burnett (1913), originally published as "Farewell Song."

____"Pain has an element of blank..." and "The heart asks pleasure first..." from "The Mystery of Pain"and "The heart asks pleasure first" by Emily Dickinson in *Poems by Emily Dickinson, First & Second Series,* Mabel Loomis Todd and T. W. Higginson, editors.

TRUE MINDS
Page 38: Title "True Minds" and sub-title "Let me not to the marriage of true minds admit impediments" from Sonnet 116 by William Shakespeare.

Page 42: "Love alters not with his brief hours and weeks/But bears it out even to the edge of doom" from Sonnet 116 by William Shakespeare.

Pages 43: "like the palm of his hand..." attributed to Albert Camus.

Page 49: "I am a wandering bark"reference to "love" as "the star to every wandering bark"from Sonnet 116 by William Shakespeare

CRUEL SUNSET
Page 51: "I will arise and go now" from "The Lake Isle at Innisfree" by W. B. Yeats.

Page 53: "To every thing there is a season..." from Ecclesiastes KJV.

SHIVA'S TABLE
Page 63: Shiva, the Hindu deity of creation and destruction, has many appellations reflecting various attributes, such as Hara (remover of sins) and Mahamaya (one of great illusion).

A Matter of Time
Page 85: "I cannot live with you…" from "In Vain" by Emily Dickinson in *Poems by Emily Dickinson, First & Second Series*, Mabel Loomis Todd and T. W. Higginson, editors.

God is Love
Page 86: "its center everywhere and circumference nowhere" paraphrased from "God is a circle whose center is everywhere and circumference nowhere," attributed to multiple sources, including Dante and St. Augustine, the earliest being Empedocles (490 - 430 BCE).

On This Ground
Page 102: "SAMUEL DE CHAMPLAIN. Due east from here…" inscription on the historic marker at Whale Cove on South Street in Rockport, Massachusetts.

Thanks & Gratitude

To my fellow writers and friends in the Finish Line Writers at Gloucester Writers Center in Gloucester, MA, for reviewing the stories in *Time and Tide* with keen insights, support, encouragement, laughter and light:
Barbara Boudreau, Stacey Dexter, Daniel Duffy, Cynthia Hendrickson, Jane Keddy, John Mullen, Cindy Schimanski.

To Coleman Barks, for his kind and generous personal permission to quote from his translation of Rumi's "A Star Without a Name" in *Say I Am You*.